THE SHARK LIST

THE
SHARK LIST

CLAY PEACHER

The Shark List

© 2025 by Clay Peacher

Editors: Anne MacDonald, Megan Mitchum
Cover and Design: Emma Elzinga

Indigo River Publishing
3 West Garden Street, Ste. 718
Pensacola, FL 32502

www.indigoriverpublishing.com

Ordering Information:

Quantity Sales: Special discounts are available on quantity purchases by corporations, associations, and others. For details, contact the publisher at the address above.

Orders by US trade bookstores and wholesalers: Please contact the publisher at the address above.

Printed in the United States of America

Library of Congress Control Number: [Insert number]
ISBN: 978-1-964686-28-8 (paperback) 978-1-964686-29-5 (ebook)

First Edition

With Indigo River Publishing, you can always expect great books, strong voices, and meaningful messages. Most importantly, you'll always find . . . *words worth reading.*

CONTENTS

PROLOGUE

Creigh and the rest of the Hammerhead Gang had a terrific upbringing in the Panhandle of Florida. The five of them were very athletic, easy on the eyes, and clever. They won back-to-back state high school football championships during their junior and senior years at Milton High School. All the boys received both academic and athletic scholarships at colleges throughout the Southeast United States, then returned to their hometown after graduation. While in their mid-teens, they were aptly named the Hammerhead Gang by the old man who taught them to shark fish along the beautiful white sandy beaches of the Gulf of Mexico. Don't be fooled by the term "gang." They could have just as easily been called the Hammerhead Five, as they were not the violent sort. They were fun, energetic, and always hung together.

After college, the Hammerhead Gang's social playground ranged from Panama City Beach, Florida, through Gulf Shores, Alabama, and all the way to New Orleans, Louisiana. They loved playing beach volleyball and frequenting the many night clubs along the beautiful

Gulf Coast. They maintained their strong bond of friendship; and their "friendly" gang activities included penalizing people for what they determined as wrongdoings. All the punishments they delivered were deserving and most were somewhat humorous.

One time, the referees in a high school basketball game changed the outcome of the game by making obvious bad calls against the home team. It was later determined that two of the three officials graduated from the visiting school, and they flagrantly helped the visitors win the game. The next week, the whistles of the cheating refs mysteriously disappeared right before game time. As a matter of fact, there were no whistles to be found anywhere on campus. In addition, the referees' striped uniforms and underwear were laced with fiberglass shards. It was quite the sight to watch the cheating officials try to referee a basketball game with no whistles, while also dealing with extreme jock itch. This is how the Hammerhead Gang rolled.

Over the next few years, the Hammerhead Gang would meet a variety of vacationers from all over the world. Most of their new friends were from southern states like Texas, Arkansas, Louisiana, Alabama, Georgia, Mississippi, and Tennessee. Occasionally, they would meet foreigners from England, Germany, Canada, and even as far away as Australia. The Hammerhead Gang enjoyed taking road trips to the hometowns of their new friends, when they could. It was a great life.

During one of their fun summer weekends, they ended up in Destin, Florida, where they met a friendly young couple from Jackson, Mississippi. Kent and Kimberly Poole were wealthy, fun, and seemingly harmless. The boys drank, danced, and laughed with Kent and Kim the entire weekend. It seemed no different from any other weekend. Little did they know, meeting this couple would change their lives forever.

The Hammerhead Gang adventures would soon expand from the Gulf Coast and surrounding states, all the way to the Virgin Islands—but these adventures were not for fun nor pleasure. These adventures would test the faith, loyalty, and strength of the Hammerhead Gang.

Come along for the exciting ride.

1

THE GREED TIRE

It was a brisk spring night in Florida's western panhandle. The stars were shining bright, and contrary to what most celebrities believe, this is the real LA—Lower Alabama. Local folks love college football, country music, and cold beer—sounds like a country song in the making, doesn't it? The sugar white beaches are beautiful, but the weather is much unlike south Florida. It can be very cold in March, but this doesn't seem to temper the spring breakers. As long as there is music, cocktails, and warm bodies, the party is on. While the college students are making their way to the panhandle, the snowbirds are headed north to escape the heat (and the kids).

The I-10 westbound lane was rather quiet on this spring night. Most of the traffic consisted of vacationers returning home from a wonderful week on the beach. Although mainly a flat highway stretching east and west across the entire state of Florida, the section of I-10 approaching Escambia Bay is elevated and provides a steep right-of-way. The area adjacent to Escambia Bay and the interstate are also very swampy and uninhabited.

Creigh and his Hammerhead Gang sat quietly at the bottom of the steep I-10 right-of-way. All five men were in their early twenties but hadn't yet outgrown their teenage immaturity. The young men were sitting on the only patch of dry land in the swamp. Nicholas and Terrance were drinking tall-boy cold beers while John-Boy and Danny were passing a reefer back-and-forth. Creigh was not partaking—he was the designated driver for the night. Their choice of, or lack of, recreational enhancers spoke volumes about their individual livelihoods.

Sooner than later, the young men became excited as they saw a large older model sedan pullover onto the right-of-way. The driver of the sedan awkwardly reversed the vehicle to a spot directly above them. Oncoming traffic on the Interstate steadily honked their horns and pointed their middle fingers at the sedan as it was careening onto the highway from time-to-time while in reverse. The vehicle had Michigan plates and the Hammerheads were certain the occupants were snowbirds—people who live in Florida during the winter and move up north for the summer.

Sure enough, an older gray-haired man emerged from the driver side door and proceeded to the back of his vehicle. Although his wife was bitching the entire time, he was focused on what looked like a brand-new tire, lying in the grass.

However, he did not realize this was an old tire, wrapped with brown grocery sacks and chalked with white chalk to look as if it were a new tire. There was a rope attached to the tire that was carefully hidden and extended to the small island inhabited by the Hammerhead Gang at the bottom of the right-of-way.

The old man struggled to loop the tire over his shoulder. After a few shrugs and adjustments, the tire felt secure. The old feller clutched the tire tightly and labored toward his vehicle. The wet grass was slippery, but he was only a few feet away from the trunk of his sedan.

In an instant, as if an external force were present, the tire was yanked from his shoulder and surged down the hill with the old man in tow. He somersaulted a couple of times before reluctantly releasing the tire. As he lay there on the wet, cold slope, he could see the tire had rolled an additional thirty feet down the hill into the swampy bottom. He knew it would be impossible to retrieve the tire by himself, and was fairly certain his wife would not be willing to help out. Still unsure of what just happened, he gathered his senses and returned to the safety of his car unharmed (except for his pride). The poor old man is probably still not sure of the events that occurred that night.

The young men waited quietly for the old man to hobble back up the hill and drive off before resetting the "greed tire" and pull rope. Once the big sedan was out of sight, the Hammerheads laughed and surmised that the old man's wife would ridicule him for the next 1,400 miles—and probably the next five years, if the truth be known. There were mixed feelings about what they had just done. Sure, they took advantage of a greedy old man, but they could have hurt him. They pulled several people down the hill that night, but none as old as the Michigan snowbird. What if he suffered a heart attack or broke a bone? Creigh was the one who pulled the rope, and it was evident he pulled much lighter for the old man, based on his short trip down the hill compared to the other greedy casualties. Terrance and Nicholas argued in favor of not pulling the old man at all. John-Boy and Danny were all about making everyone pay for their greed. Lucky for the old man, it was not John-Boy nor Danny's turn to pull the rope. The boys placed the tire back on the side of the Interstate, hid the pull rope in the tall grass and stretched it all the way down to their swamp island hiding place. The Gang quickly agreed to no more tire pulling of "old people."

Still arguing about the most recent tire pulling, the boys did not notice their newest "greed tire" victim easing into the emergency lane. As the occupant got out of the car, an oncoming eighteen-wheeler's headlights revealed a very distinctly dressed driver and vehicle. It was a white and green four-door sedan with a line of blue lights mounted on the top of the car stretching from the driver's door to the passenger side door.

The man exiting the cruiser was large in stature, wearing a cowboy hat and boots. His badge shined brightly each time a car passed by. He was none other than Deputy Delay. Delay was an old school law officer and unbeknownst to him, the boys knew him well. The Hammerhead Gang had outsmarted Deputy Delay on many occasions over the past several years. However, tonight might prove different.

Sure, this section of I-10 was out of his jurisdiction, but Delay was not going to pass up a "brand spanking new" tire. Unfortunately for Deputy Delay, he did not meet the "old people" criteria that the Hammerhead Gang had just established. It was John-Boy's turn to pull the rope and the other boys knew he was not going to back down. The Deputy, displaying the same greed as his predecessors, briefly looked each direction, looped the tire over his shoulder and headed toward his patrol car. He was grinning from ear to ear. Delay was looking forward to showing off his newfound treasure to his fellow deputies.

"Don't do it!" whispered Creigh. "Let him go."

John-Boy looked at Creigh with that shit-eating grin Creigh had seen many times. John-Boy nodded his head and made a slight gesture as if he were going to drop the rope.

Creigh sighed in relief.

Deputy Delay had only taken about three steps when the rope tightened, and John-Boy gave it a violent tug. The tug was so powerful that it dislocated Deputy Delay's shoulder. The highly decorated law officer fell backward and tumbled all the way to the bottom of the hill, settling in the wet marsh. It was very dark, and he was no more than fifteen feet from the Hammerhead Gang. Deputy Delay was on all fours in knee deep swamp water, gasping as if he were in the early stages of a heart attack. The boys were strategically located on the only dry spot in the swamp—a small island the size of a minivan that was heavily hidden with marsh wetland plants. Like the old snowbird, Delay was confused. Unlike the old snowbird, Delay had a huge gash on his right knee and a horrific pain in his right shoulder. Immediately upon his landing in the swamp, the frogs stopped croaking and the area fell silent. Delay scanned the unfamiliar environment and could only see darkness. Once he realized this was no accident, he feared another attack was imminent and began scrambling up the hill while radioing for backup. The Gang knew he was injured by his cursing, screaming, and moaning—and the fact that he left the tire behind! His knee was bleeding profusely and would certainly require a hefty number of stitches.

It would be a short matter of time before the place was crawling with law enforcement. Santa Rosa County Sheriff's office was known for emptying the donut shop to remove a cat from a tree. This was assault on an officer. Heck, they might call-in backup from Escambia and Okaloosa counties as well. The boys turned due east and starting hopping, one by one, across the swamp water. It looked as if they were walking on top of the swamp water. Deputy Delay could hear the movement but was unsure if it were a retreat or he was being circle stalked. After all, what had just happened to him? He continued to scurry up the hill and call for backup. Out of breath, scared, dirty, embarrassed, and in deep pain, Delay made it to his cruiser. He would have to explain to his superiors why he was parked on the side of the Interstate and conducting business out of his jurisdiction.

The boys exited the swamp onto solid ground and immediately

picked up a narrow, winding trail for almost a quarter of a mile. At the end of the trail was a swift flowing, north-to-south creek. On the edge of the six-foot-deep creek was a well-built wooden raft, held afloat by four thirty-gallon plastic drums. The boys huddled on the raft and Creigh untethered a rope that was attached to a nearby tree. The raft moved swiftly under the Interstate through a large dark culvert. The raft was bouncing and accelerating in a manner where any sudden side-to-side shift in weight would be catastrophic. This would terrify most people because Mulat Creek was known for an overpopulation of water moccasins and alligators, but the boys stayed quiet and steady. Suddenly, in the scary dark culvert, the raft came to a crashing stop. The raft had collided with a flimsy, stand-alone piling protruding vertically in the middle of the creek. The collision jolted the boys and caused the raft to slowly pivot 180 degrees. The boys remained quiet and steady. After the raft completed the pivot, it started to build up speed again. By this time, the raft had made it through the Interstate culvert and was near enough to the shoreline that the boys could easily jump to the safety of dry land. They were now on the south side of the Interstate and a safe distance to the east of the greed tire escapade. The empty raft safely came to a rest about thirty yards downstream. A narrow trail led them an additional 200 yards to a dim dirt road where Nicholas's old Land Shark was parked. His car was named the Land Shark because of the boys' passion for shark fishing. Nicholas had even exchanged the hood ornament for a large shark fin.

Without speaking, the boys loaded the rope and greed tire into the trunk, piled into the vehicle and quietly drove off. As they crossed the Interstate, they could see the congregation of emergency vehicles—police cars, firetrucks, an ambulance, and even a K-9 unit. The boys stayed quiet and steady. As they made it back to their neighborhood, each sported a slight grin. Maybe this was not what most men in their early twenties did for entertainment, but this was a typical night for the Hammerhead Gang.

2

MEET THE
HAMMERHEAD GANG

On a hot, muggy, Florida night, what could be more exciting and fun than 'greedy tire pulling'? The only answer for these boys is shark hunting. Yes, the truth is that this outdoor sport is really fishing, but the boys thought it was super cool to call it shark hunting. Their favorite place to hunt for sharks was a natural deep crater in the Gulf of Mexico about a mile offshore, in between Navarre Beach and Pensacola Beach. It was called the seven-mile hole because of its unusual depth (about twenty feet deeper than the surrounding Gulf seabed), and it was exactly seven miles east of the famous, but long-gone, Tikki Lounge on Pensacola Beach. The deep hole and limestone rock provided shelter for all sorts of sea life, including a variety of man-eating sharks. Hammerheads, Bulls, Tigers, and Makos were caught on a routine basis. On any given night, there would be a dozen fishermen sitting on the beach at the seven-mile hole, waiting for their reel to scream with a monster shark on the other end of the line.

The boys learned about shark hunting at an early age from a salty old shark fisherman named Elmo. The boys never knew Elmo's last name, nor where he lived, but he was a resident of the seven-mile hole beach on most nights. Legend had it that a shark killed Elmo's wife forty years earlier and he vowed to kill every shark in the Gulf. Elmo never spoke of his wife and the boys certainly did not want to question the story. Over the years, Elmo caught thousands of sharks and taught the Gang how to rig lines, thread baits, select the best fishing times, and how to handle the ferocious beast once they were brought to shore. All of these were lessons that the boys would never forget. In turn, the boys would bring Elmo snacks and drinks on each visit to the seven-mile hole. Elmo took a liking to the young men and it was him that gave them their title, "Hammerhead Gang." The young men loved the name and fished right alongside Elmo, until he just wasn't there anymore. Danny's dad told the boys that Elmo drowned in an accident doing what he loved, but the boys knew in their hearts that he got tired of waiting and purposely walked out into the Gulf to be with his wife. RIP Elmo.

Creigh, John-Boy, Nicholas, Terrance, and Danny were the founding and only members of the Hammerhead Gang. They had been best buddies since the second grade. They played together and against each other in organized sports while growing up. They competed in almost every facet of life. Whether it was playing baseball, basketball, football, track, or seeing who could catch the most oak leaves on a windy day—these boys competed. Sometimes it would end in a fight, someone crying, or going home mad. The next day, they would patch things up and start all over again.

As they grew older, they learned to compete together as a team. When the boys were in high school, the Mighty Milton Panthers won back-to-back state football championships. The Hammerhead Gang was an enormous key to the team's success. These Panthers were the first football state champions in the history of Santa Rosa County and, by default, the boys became something like celebrities. All five members of the Hammerhead Gang were recruited by college sports teams. Four members played on the defensive side of the football field. John-Boy was the only member that played offense.

John-Boy played tight end on the football team. He was also a state champion swimmer and a standout basketball player for the Mighty Panthers. John-Boy was certainly a rebel and walked to his own beat. He only played football because his older brother made him. John-Boy really did not seem to care about the outcome of any of the football games. As a matter of fact, he really did not care about the outcome of anything in life. One time, the Panthers were in a nip and tuck football game and with only a few seconds remaining, John-Boy made an unbelievable, crazy, acrobatic touchdown catch to win the game. A week later, people asked him about the catch and he could not recall even playing in the game. There is a good chance that recreational drugs played a role in his memory lapse. As great as he was at swimming, John-Boy was only on the swim team to look at pretty girls in bathing suits. Now, basketball was a different story. Apart from chasing women, he was only passionate about basketball. He could tell you about every basket, every blocked shot, and every rebound. It was mind boggling how in-tune and well-versed he was with the things he liked.

The Panther basketball team consisted of twelve white players and a Black manager. The manager's name was Rooster, who was a very popular student on campus. Before each game, the players would rub Rooster's head for good luck. It seemed to work as the undersized, over-matched Panthers posted winning seasons every year in basketball.

John-Boy had the look of a male model. He was tall, dark, and handsome. He was always the ladies' choice. His brother was the quarterback of the first state championship football team. He took care of John-Boy when he got into trouble. While he did not approve of the antics of the Hammerhead Gang, he turned a blind eye as long as they made good grades and helped the team win championships.

One time, Creigh asked John-Boy a simple question about his home life and John-Boy quietly turned and walked away. For well over a year, he would not talk to Creigh or any of the Hammerhead Gang members. Then one day, John-Boy showed up at Creigh's house as if nothing had ever happened. This was certainly not confirmation of anything in particular, but it was confirmation that something occurred in John-Boy's childhood that was different from the other boys.

Over the years, Milton High School football was known for stout defense and the championship years were no exception. The Panthers shutout seven of their opponents in route to their last State Title. Their coach, Hurley Manning, was old school and instilled discipline and work ethic in all the boys (except John-Boy). Creigh and Terrance were all-state linebackers. Both of these young men signed college football scholarships and played at a high level.

Creigh was the unchosen leader of the Hammerhead Gang. He planned out most of the adventures and kept them out of trouble. He seemed to have a knack for anticipating how things would go down. Creigh was tall with blond hair and blue eyes. He made decent grades throughout high school, but this did not nearly reflect his intelligence level. Creigh was smart— *really* smart. He scored a thirty on the ACT college entrance exam, despite the fact that he stayed out 'til after 4 a.m. the night before. Creigh's father was a three-sport athlete at a small college in west Alabama and was now a Florida Fish and Wildlife Officer. His mother was the daughter of a poor farmer in Hattiesburg, Mississippi. She taught English and coached softball at Milton High School. His parents worked hard, and he had a solid family life. Creigh was the youngest of four siblings and, like typical youngest siblings, his parents were much more lenient on him. They did not discipline him as they did their three older children.

All the boys loved to hunt and fish, but Terrance took it to a much higher level. He would hunt before school, fish after ball practice, and talk about it with anyone that would listen. Most of the time, he smelled like a cross between a speckled trout and a dead deer—if that is possible.

The other boys joked with Terrance all the time about his unusually large head. Back in the day, prior to football season each year, the High School Football Equipment Manager would have to order a special helmet for Terrance. The head jokes never ceased but Terrance did not mind. He was happy-go-lucky and could always be counted on to make someone smile—even in the worst of times. Terrance was a very trustworthy, loyal friend.

Danny played defensive back on the high school football team and was also a stellar third basemen on the baseball team. Danny's parents were separated, and Danny lived with his father, who was a janitor at a local high school. His mother was addicted to prescription drugs and was rarely in his life. Danny was not the biggest in size but was the most athletic of all the boys. If someone challenged Danny in any sport, they would likely end up on the wrong end of a butt-whooping. Danny went to a JUCO on a baseball scholarship and from there was an early pick in the professional baseball draft. He played a few years in the minor leagues and eventually burned out due to the lengthy baseball schedule and long bus rides.

Danny and John-Boy seemed to think alike and stick together most of the time.

Nicholas was the biggest of the Hammerhead Gang. He played defensive line on the football team and was known for his bizarre antics.

One time, prior to the first state championship semi-final playoff game, he bit off the head of a frog in front of all the coaches and players. The audience was not sure what it symbolized, but it worked. The Mighty Milton Panthers won 41 – 0. Nicholas also played Division I Football and competed on the track team as a Discus Thrower, Hammer Thrower, and Shot Putter. During the summer months, Nicholas would drink a gallon of milk...everyday! He was one big, strong feller.

According to the other Hammerheads, Nicholas's most important contribution was his car. The Land Shark was dependable and transported these guys all the time. Fishing trips, beach trips, and partying trips—all accomplished in the Land Shark.

If it wasn't clear before, it certainly should be now. This was not an average group of young men. All the Hammerhead Gang made outstanding grades throughout high school and college. They were well liked by their teachers, classmates, and community. All five members were strong, healthy, and good-looking—by most standards. The Hammerhead Gang was a close-knit group and very few people, if any, understood their bond and knew of their adventures. They were not out to hurt innocent people, but they found great pleasure, almost a necessity, in dishing out just deserts. Relating to the aforementioned "greed tire escapade," they may have stretched the boundaries a tad bit between right, wrong, and greedy.

A better example of how the Hammerhead Gang operated occurred several years earlier while still in high school. An older boy, Dusty, beat-up Booger Boy Billy Davidson for no apparent reason. Booger Boy Billy was a science nerd who picked his nose on a regular basis (hence the name) and was incapable of defending himself. Booger Boy Billy ended up with a black eye, broken ribs, and low self-esteem. This was totally uncalled for, and the second time that Dusty had brutally beaten Billy that year. The Hammerhead Gang silently vowed to get justice for little Billy. A few weeks after the beating, Milton High School had a dog and drug search. The Hammerhead Gang was aware of the search because Nicholas's dad was a city cop. Imagine the shock on ole Dusty's face when a small bag of marijuana was pulled from his locker. Yes, he was a pot smoker and had gotten away with it for years—but he just could not recall placing that small bag of pot in his locker. Dusty was expelled from school and little Billy was never happier. Booger Boy Billy would never know how the boys had made his life easier by placing the small bag of marijuana in Dusty's locker. This is how the Hammerhead Gang rolled.

By the way, it was no accident that the "greed tire escapade" worked flawlessly. The boys chose that particular location along the Interstate because of the steep hill, the swamp, and the small island. The tire was positioned so it could easily be seen by oncoming traffic and the pull rope would be hidden in the tall grass. The appearance of the boys walking on water during their escape from the swamp was possible due to well-anchored milk crates just below the water's surface. The two dim trails were only accessible by someone who knew where the secret entrances were located. The raft, the vertical piling in the middle of the creek that steered them to shore, and the location of the getaway car, the Land Shark, were all part of their perfect planning. The boys went an unnecessary step further by placing a life-sized blow-up doll and dirty magazines at the edge of the swamp. Why? It would be difficult for Deputy Delay or any other "greed tire" victim to explain to the authorities or even their wives why they were in the swamp—especially since there was no new tire, or suspects. Only a blow-up doll was present! These young men were good. *Real* good.

3

SHARK HUNTING

The heat crawled on their damp skin, the humidity of the southern summer air leaving a sheen of sweat on their bodies, but they barely noticed as their eyes pierced through the black night across the Gulf of Mexico. Any moment now the thin but stout braided line would flicker, then pull tight, and the game was on. Creigh crouched in the sand, his fingers mindlessly playing with the wet grains. For him, the biggest draw to the hunt was the silence, the feeling of calm that washed over him as the Gulf waves licked at his toes. He knew it was different for the others.

"C'mon man, ain't nothin' bitin' tonight. Let's get our drank-on and hit a few nightclubs before it is too late." John-Boy's voice echoed through the night and crawled at Creigh's serenity.

He flicked the last pieces of sand from his hand before standing to turn to John-Boy, who was only visible by the camp lantern hanging on one of the fishing poles.

"You can get drunk here," Creigh assured him, nodding at Danny to toss his buddy a beer.

"Yeah, John-Boy, chill out, we are huntin' tonight," Danny added.

The seven-mile hole was unusually quiet on this particular night. There were only a couple of other fishermen and they appeared to be targeting pompano and whiting. This made the odds much better for the Hammerhead Gang to land a nice shark.

The Hammerhead Gang's fishing tackle was far less than adequate. Prior to the previous summer, the young shark slayers pooled their money together and purchased two medium shark fishing reels and two large shark fishing reels. The boys purchased all four rusted reels and matching rods at local garage sales and flea markets. Although fine fishing equipment by their standards, the equipment was too small. Some nights, the boys and their shark hunting gear were no match for the monstrous sharks.

Two-inch diameter PVC spikes were deeply driven into the sand and made nice, sturdy anchors for each of the rod-n-reel combos. They were spread out far enough to not become tangled but close enough to be monitored by everyone.

Suddenly, one of the fishing reels started making a loud clicking noise.

"Look! Look! Look!" cried Terrance as he scrambled up from the sand, reaching for the shark reel. He switched the reel drag into gear which made the line tighten and the fishing pole bend to a point where the tip was almost touching the beach sand at the edge of the surf.

"Hell yeah!" Danny whooped, slapping at his knee, "It's a big one!"

Terrance was now fully strapped to the fishing rod and reel by a harness that was wrapped around his torso.

"Damn! It's powerful!" Terrance shouted.

Terrance held the rod with both hands. The butt of the rod was painfully digging into his thigh. He tried to reel in the line but for every inch he gained, he lost four to the shark. "Damn rod is gonna break," he hissed. He used his body as leverage to pull back on the rod, but it did not help. The monstrous shark was still in control.

"Let it be, man!" Creigh shouted.

Terrance eased up on the reel drag, allowing the shark to pull the line out into the darkness. The shark swam further and further away. This provoked cussing and bickering from all the boys. Creigh placed a "gut bucket" around Terrance's waist so the rod butt would not dig into his thigh. He ignored the cursing and bickering from the other boys and stayed focused on the battle. This went on for about ten minutes and allowed Terrance time to catch his breath.

"Now!" Creigh instructed. Terrance tightened the drag lever on the reel. The pole bent sharply but the fishing line was no longer unspooling from the reel. Terrance pulled back on the rod and then reeled in the line as he moved the rod forward. He "pumped back" and "reeled forward" for about twenty grueling minutes. He was finally seeing some progress for his efforts.

All of a sudden, the line went limp.

Creigh yelled, "Reel faster, reel faster!!"

Terrance was pissed, thinking he had lost the monster shark. He reluctantly but frantically followed Creigh's orders and reeled in line as fast as possible. Suddenly the line became tight, and it was evident that the massive shark was still hooked.

"Obviously, the shark was swimming toward the shoreline, causing the line to go limp. This allows the shark an opportunity to shake loose the hook," said Creigh.

"Only big sharks know that trick," chimed in Nicholas.

All the boys agreed.

The cat-n-mouse game went on for almost an hour. The massive shark would pull out the line and then Terrance would regain the line.

Terrance was exhausted and his buddies continued to rehydrate him with fluids (including beer) and pour cold water on his head.

All the boys knew their roles in this process.

On this night, Terrance was obviously on the rod; Nicholas was his emotional support and the person to keep him hydrated; Creigh was his coach; Danny was in knee deep water and was the spotter. It was his job to locate the beast as it got closer to the shore. John-Boy's job was to stay out of the way.

Suddenly Danny screamed. "We got color! We got color!"

This meant he could see the massive body of the shark.

Creigh and Nicholas each grabbed heavy ropes that were already rigged for noosing the giant shark. The noose had to be big enough to fit over the shark's tail.

They cautiously waded into the water on each side of Danny.

"It's a Greater Hammerhead! It's a Greater Hammerhead!" exclaimed Danny. "The shark is at least twelve feet long! I'll try to make him turn parallel to the shore! Whichever one of you is closest to the tail, lasso him and pull the rope tight."

"What does parallel mean?" asked John-Boy. His question obviously fell on deaf ears.

Right on cue, the massive shark turned sideways, and the tail was directly in front of Nicholas.

"Rope'em, Nicky! Rope'em!" shouted Creigh.

Nicholas, now in waist-deep water, quickly but cautiously looped the large noose over the Greater Hammerhead's tail and pulled it tight.

In an instant, the giant shark whipped its tail, hitting Nicholas in the chest and knocking him closer to the shark's mouth. This is a feeding method shared by alligators, crocodiles, and yes, man-eating sharks.

Nicholas dropped the end of the rope, dazed from the blow he just took.

Creigh threw his rope at the shark's head in an attempt to distract the big beast.

At the same time, Danny grabbed Nicholas and pulled him away from danger.

The shark was still hooked and now much angrier. Terrance continued to keep a taut line on the shark.

"The noose is still around his tail!" shouted Terrance.

All of the Gang were standing ankle-deep in the surf and contemplating what to do.

By now, Nicholas had regained his senses and was equally as angry as the shark. He could see the end of the noose rope trailing behind the shark. Before discussing their options, Nicholas charged out into the water, directly at the shark.

"What the hell are you doing, Nicholas!?" screamed Creigh.

Suddenly the shark took another tail swipe at Nicholas but he was prepared this time. Nicholas jumped back and the shark missed. This tail swipe flung the loose end of the noose rope directly to Nicholas. He grabbed the end of the rope and immediately turned toward shore. He was grunting and screaming but not making much progress.

"How 'bout a lil' frickin' help!" he yelled.

Creigh and Danny reluctantly entered the shark's habitat and grabbed a spot on the rope. All three boys slowly walked backward toward the beach. As much as Terrance wanted to help his buddies pull the rope, he remained on the reel, as Elmo had taught them.

The big shark did not like being pulled backward and violently started twisting in the water. It was a twenty-minute real-life tug-of-war contest between men and beast. They were dangerously close to the uncontrollable shark. Although completely exhausted, they were finally able to bring the shark safely to shore.

Terrance secured the fishing equipment and ran over to celebrate the victory. The trio of ropers were laying on their backs in the sand, but each managed a high-five to Terrance.

"That was cool, dudes," said John-Boy.

The foursome rolled their eyes in unison. They were angry at John-Boy for not helping, but this was typical of him. Besides, they had just caught their biggest shark ever and there was plenty of night left to catch another one.

"Ya'll ready to catch anther one?" asked Creigh.

"Might as well," said Terrance. "It's too late to go to a nightclub and besides, we all smell like fish chum."

"I don't smell like chum," said John-Boy.

As usual, the Gang ignored him and began rigging their rods and reels.

Shark hunting from the beach is not easy. The biggest challenge is placing bait, usually a dead Bonita caught from one of the local piers, out far enough to be appetizing for a shark. Some of the shark fishermen would wade out to chest-deep water and then sling the bait, like an Olympic track and field Hammer Thrower.

The Hammerhead Gang wanted to out-fish all the other fishermen at the seven-mile hole. To do this, their baits needed to be further out into the Gulf to what they thought was the shark's primary stalking grounds. Little did they know that sharks can roam for hundreds of miles. They can be thirty feet from shore or ten miles from shore in a matter of a few hours. Nonetheless, they would rock, paper, scissors to determine who would have to carry out the baits. The loser would have to rig all four baits, strap the baits to a surfboard and paddle out a country mile into the Gulf. He, the loser, would then drop off the baits approximately a hundred yards apart, east to west, and paddle back in. Keep in mind, this is all being accomplished in the dark of night and sometimes the surf conditions were very rough. Every so often, the bait hauler, or haulers, would fall from the surfboard into the bloodied waters of the Gulf of Mexico.

"Hey, remember that time Nicholas fell off the surfboard?" John-Boy cackled. "Man, you had to swim a mile back to shore."

"Yeah, no thanks to you idiots." Nicholas narrowed his eyes at John-Boy, the one person in the group who had the swimming skills to save him, but just stood on the beach haggling him to swim faster and that there was a shark fin coming up behind him.

All the boys took exception to being called idiots, but Nicholas was one big dude and probably not the guy to pick a fight with.

"Ah man, you were fine," John-Boy slapped his back too hard. Nicholas winced. John-Boy was not his favorite person, especially after that night. He knew John-Boy was not like the others. He could depend on the others. They had each other's backs, but not John-Boy. He only looked out for himself.

John-Boy was referring to an occasion when Terrance and Nicholas were teaming up to set baits when Terrance fell from his surfboard and subsequently lost it to the mighty waves of the Gulf of Mexico. Nicholas paddled over to help Terrance but subsequently lost his surfboard too, due to Terrance franticly trying to climb on his board. It was a full moon and both men, board-less, had to swim to shore in the shark-infested water. Although Terrance and Nicholas were exhausted, they made it to shore without further incident. They both swore they saw multiple shark fins on their journey to land. Within the next three hours, the Gang caught four sharks—one being a ten-foot Hammerhead. At that time, it was their biggest one ever! Maybe their tale of seeing shark fins was accurate.

Another great thing about shark fishing was that the boys' girlfriends approved of it and would allow them to stay out all night as long as they were going shark fishing. On occasion, the boys would pack the ole Land Shark with their shark hunting gear and say bye to their girlfriends. Instead of shark hunting, they would venture out on a partying road trip to Panama City Beach, Destin, or Gulf Shores. These young men were slick and knew how to have a good time.

"Let's call it a night," said Creigh. "You guys sound like a bunch of bickering sorority girls. Besides, the wind is starting to pick up."

The boys grumbled at his statement but, like clockwork, turned and faced the Gulf, raised their beers and in unison said, "To Elmo" and then chugged 'em down. This was a tradition they started to honor their shark hunting hero.

The Hammerhead Gang gathered up their shark hunting gear, beach chairs, ice chest, and surfboards. They slowly trudged across the beach toward the Land Shark.

Once they crossed the sand dunes, they could see John-Boy perched on the hood of the car.

"Took y'all long enough," said John-Boy.

"Get the hell off my car! You are gonna dent my hood!" shouted Nicholas.

With that, John-Boy raised his hands in surrender and crawled off the car.

Nicholas dropped all his gear and shoved John-Boy to the oyster shell right-of-way. John-Boy grimaced in pain but still snickered at Nicholas.

"That looked painful," said Terrance.

"But deserving," said Creigh.

Stinking to high heaven, the boys piled into the car and made their journey home.

4

THE DREADED
SHARK LIST

As the weekend came to a close, and morning threatened to end the night, Creigh sat in his filthy living room, drinking whiskey on the rocks—his usual. He offered a sip to John-Boy, who was beyond stoned already, but still going strong, as always.

"Man, what are we doin' here?" Creigh pondered.

"Living the dream, gettin' stoned and chasing women," replied John-Boy.

"There's gotta be more to life than just this," said Creigh.

John-Boy shook his head. "We still got it, brother."

Creigh sunk deeper into the couch they'd found on the side of the road. It was infested with fleas, the obvious reason it had been discarded.

"We used to stand for something," he mumbled. "We used to be something."

His voice faded into the background as his eyes flickered before everything went dark. Suddenly, Creigh was lost in the past, his dreams taking over as he bounced from proudly walking the halls of his high school to hanging out with his football teammates at the college campus union. He could not shake the feeling that he'd peaked in life. He no longer played ball; he was poor by most standards; he currently did not have a girlfriend; his buddies in the Hammerhead Gang were always busy; and most of all, they had totally ignored the Shark List.

The Shark List was a treasured document that was only shared within the Hammerhead Gang. Ironically, the Shark List had nothing to do with shark hunting. The Hammerhead Gang maintained a list of people who deserved reprimand for any reason that did not sit well with them. The Gang acted as the judge, jury, and punishment enforcer. Their goal was not necessarily to hurt someone, but to make them feel as if there were consequences for everything in life. In a round-about way, it was a way of enforcing karma.

There were many ways to make the Shark List, the main one being if someone hurt or embarrassed a member of the Hammerhead Gang. This was automatic placement onto the Shark List. Friends or family members of the Hammerhead Gang were also protected by this automatic placement. On occasion, someone might make the list by doing something harmful to the community or harmful to an unknown, innocent person. Over the years, dozens of people made the Shark List. The only way a person was removed from the list is if they corrected their wrongdoing or suffered the wrath of the Hammerhead Gang. Thus, Dusty, the pot smoking bully who hurt Booger Boy Billy, was removed from the Shark List once he was expelled from school.

The Shark List was growing, and the Hammerhead Gang had less and less time to address the wrong doers. There was the opposing team's coach that was reportedly spying on their Alma Mater's football practices; there was the County Commissioner that wanted to raise taxes and give all the Commissioners a raise; there was a pesky neighbor, ole Mr. Gurkey, who accused the boys of ringing his doorbell and running.

This childish act had been going on for years and years. Mr. Gurkey was correct on his assumption of this childish act, but he had no proof. Regardless, he told-on the boys and subsequently made the Shark List.

The largest group by numbers on the Shark List was by far the Santa Rosa County Women's Club (SRCWC), that wanted to ban high school football in Santa Rosa County, because it was violent and inhumane. The SRCW Club consisted of twenty snobby-nosed, well-to-do ladies that had nothing better to do with their time. They wanted to convert high school football from tackle football to flag football. The truth be known, their kids and grandkids were not tough enough to play tackle football. Every year, they would propose this change to the County Commissioners and every year it would be voted down. There was a real fear that one day they would get the votes needed to abolish tackle football. This was lame and these ladies certainly deserved some type of Shark List punishment.

The aforementioned were just a handful of the unlucky patrons on the Shark List. The Shark List had become Creigh's legacy—more so than all the football championships combined. The Shark List was maintained by all the members of the Hammerhead Gang and was NEVER to be shared with an outsider. The Shark List was the place not to be.

A few hours later, Creigh's eyes flashed open, his entire body jolting to life. He was no longer in dream land. A single thread of light peaked through the blackout curtains across the living room. John-Boy was still passed out beside Creigh on the couch. The couch fleas were very active this morning. Creigh surmised that they were drawn to John-Boy.

"I have to get my life together," Creigh sighed, rubbing his hands over his dry, tired face forcing himself to wake up. The harsh reminder of his dream, of the person he once was, felt as if someone had ignited a fire inside of Creigh. He wanted his life to mean something again, to be important. He needed to get his crap together and figure it out.

Turning to John-Boy, he determined that he was going to move out as soon as possible. Living with John-Boy was a mistake. He needed to find a better job, or maybe go back to school. Do something, anything. He splashed water on his face, over and over, thinking it might make things clearer. Instead, it only made a mess on the bathroom floor. *Today I'm going to turn it around*, he told himself. *Today is going to be different.*

Soon, the Gang was present, and the boys were headed to the high school gym for a muscle pump prior to hitting the beach. Although they graduated from high school and college several years ago, they were still allowed to use the high school weight room and gym. There are privileges that come with winning two state championships. As they drove past the bus ramp, they noticed what look like a stack of boxes—the green and white low-profile boxes used for fundraising donut sales. They whipped around and got out to investigate. Sure enough, there were about ten boxes of glazed donuts, there for the pickin'.

As usual, Terrance and Nicholas, the conservative Hammerheads, wanted nothing to do with stealing donuts; John-Boy and Danny, the wildest Hammerheads, were already wolfing-down a pair of glazed donuts. The boys decided to compromise and only take one box to share prior to their workout.

As they were leaving, an older lady appeared from behind the band building. The nice lady informed the boys that, as they assumed, the donuts were for a Milton High School band fundraiser and a couple of the band members forgot to pick up their donuts. She said the boys could have all ten boxes and the band members would be responsible for the cost.

Free donuts? Are you kidding? The boys decided to skip their workout and just eat donuts. The Gang devoured nearly three boxes of donuts while riding around the quaint little town of Milton, Florida. Nicholas was chauffeuring the Gang in the ole Land Shark when a supersized stretch sedan pulled out directly in front of them, causing Nicholas to slam on brakes and jolt everyone in the car. The donuts tumbled off the seat and spilled onto the dirty floorboard of his car. The stretch sedan was now directly in front of the boys. Nicholas whipped around the car, ready for a confrontation, only to find one of the snooty ole Santa Rosa County Women's Club divas, Miss Ida, driving the vehicle. She looked at him as if he had done something wrong. Then she sped off.

"You F'N bitch!" shouted Danny.

The other boys cursed Miss Ida as well.

"Maybe we should put her on the Shark List separate from the Women's Club!" said Nicholas.

Suddenly, Creigh jumped from his seat and exclaimed, "I got it!!"

The rest of the boys knew it was going to be something good because Creigh never got that excited. Creigh directed Nicholas to a local convenience store where Creigh ran in and purchased a couple of adult magazines. The boys were puzzled and thought that maybe Creigh had been hit in the head one too many times in football.

Soon after, the boys unloaded at Creigh's apartment. Creigh directed all of them to relax and enjoy the magazines while he gathered all the towels from the bathroom closet. Still thinking Creigh had gone crazy, the boys did not mind because they were already engaged in the magazines to the point of arousal. He then asked each of them to take off all their clothes and to grab a towel. By now, the boys were sure that Creigh had lost his mind. What on earth were they doing?

Creigh, naked himself, brought in the boxes of donuts and demanded each member take a couple of donuts. By then, Danny and Terrance had figured it out and were dying laughing. John-Boy and Nicholas were still clueless and now thought all the other Gang members had lost their minds.

Creigh asked each boy to thread as many donuts as possible onto the only digit-like body part besides fingers and toes and then wrap the towel around their head so no one could recognize them. They were all cracking up at this point. Most of the boys could hold three or four donuts but Nicholas easily held seven. Creigh set up the timer on his camera and snapped the picture.

The boys knew that Miss Ida and the snooty Women's Club were meeting at ten o'clock so they had to hurry. On the way, the boys drafted a note:

> Dear Ladies,
>
> Thank you for all that you do for our community. We hope to come to an agreement on the Football situation at the next County Commissioner meeting. Please enjoy the donuts and we hope to see you soon.
>
> Sincerely,
>
> County Commissioners, District 1A

Danny and Terrance were neatly placing the donuts back in the boxes. Nicholas was still bragging about his donut holding stature. Although impressed, the other boys were tired of hearing about it. Nicholas parked the Land Shark about two blocks from the Women's Club. Creigh wiped down the boxes and taped the note to the top box.

There was no doubt who would deliver the donuts. John-Boy tightened his hoodie around his face and grabbed the stacked boxes of donuts. He quietly placed the fresh donuts on the porch of the SRCWC building and returned to the car. The boys completed the task with forty-five minutes to spare.

The Hammerhead Gang went back to Creigh's apartment. Creigh, electronically ahead of his time, had recently purchased a portable color printer. Creigh printed an 8 x 10 photo of the face-hidden, donut-threaded, aroused young men and placed it in an envelope addressed to the Women's Club. He would drop the envelope in a public mailbox later in the evening. The women of the SRCWC are in for a nice surprise today...and a bigger surprise later in the week!

Creigh sighed and said to himself. "Scratch the Santa Rosa Women's Club from the Shark List. I guess I will wait 'til tomorrow to turn my life around."

5

THE O-T-T

When Creigh was fourteen, he met a sweet young southern girl from the great state of Alabama. Sydney vacationed each summer on the sugar white beaches of Navarre, Florida. Her father owned one of the largest manufacturing corporations in the south and her uncle was a larger-than-life political figure in the state of Alabama. As could be expected, they owned one of the most beautiful beach cottages on Navarre Beach. The cottage, or better described as a château, was three stories tall and could be divided into three separate living quarters. The top two floors were for family members and special guests. On the second floor, each bedroom had a football theme—one was Alabama, one was Auburn, and the other was Georgia Tech. The third floor had a marine life theme—one bedroom had Billfish mounts, one had Pelagic fish paintings, and the third had bottom fish, such as grouper, snapper, and amberjack. Above the third floor, there was an observation deck and four telescopes that were rumored to be surplus from the space center in Huntsville, Alabama. In all, the top two floors could sleep sixteen people comfortably. The bottom floor was used for storage of fishing gear, beach chairs, umbrellas, and such. Occasionally, the bottom floor was used to house babysitters, undesirable guests, and people like Creigh. The top floors were immaculate and fit for royalty. The bottom floor was nice but unkempt. Creigh never recalled seeing a family member in the bottom floor.

Creigh and Sydney would spend as many summer days as possible playing in the surf or just walking on the beach. Creigh jokingly teased Sydney all the time about being a redneck from Alabama.

In rebuttal, Sydney reminded Creigh that the Panhandle of Florida was really just an extension of "Lower Alabama." She also reminded him of things like the incredible college football teams in the state of Alabama; the fact that windshield wipers were invented in Alabama; more snails resided in Alabama than any other state; and Alabama was the first state to recognize Christmas as an official holiday.

Sydney was, by far, much better at trivia than Creigh. Little did Creigh know, she invested much of her time researching good Alabama trivia and bad Florida trivia prior to her visits to Florida. It was all good fun.

At night, Creigh and Sydney would lay on the beach, staring at the sky, attempting to name the different stars and galaxies. Sydney was also much better at naming the stars, but Creigh did not care—all he wanted was to be beside Sydney. Although they never kissed, there was a bond established between these two young teenagers that would last a lifetime.

Sydney and her family usually stayed at Navarre Beach for roughly four weeks of the summer season. The house would remain vacant for the remainder of the year. Sydney's dad took a liking to Creigh and gave him a set of keys to the place in case there was ever an emergency. This was an enormous responsibility for Creigh, and he did not take it lightly. He kept the keys a secret and spoke of this key deal to no one. Over the course of many years, Creigh had only been called twice to check on the house; both times were after a hurricane in which the house faired quite well. One hot summer day, the Hammerhead Gang was playing "Jungle Rules Beach Volleyball." For those who do not know, JRBV is where anything goes. Players can crash the net, have full contact with the other team's players, carry, double hit, curse, spit, or even fight. The rule was: there is no rules. Most teams played with six members. Some played with more. The Hammerhead Gang only played with five players. The Hammerhead Gang were the kings of the beach in JRBV.

On this particular day, the competition was exceptionally good. There were made-up teams of vacationers from Georgia, Tennessee, and Kentucky. The local Air Force Base and Navy Base also had teams comprised of strapping young military men. The only way to stay on the court is to win. The Hammerhead Gang did not take losing lightly. The temperature was a sweltering 100 degrees and the boys were sweating profusely. There was no slacking today. The boys had to play at a top level in each and every game. After six hours of Jungle Ball, the Gang finished the day exhausted, but undefeated.

As one might expect, a group of Cajun girls from Thibodaux, Louisiana, were in town and had become quite the fans of the hometown favorite team. Although it was not Louisiana's spring break, this group of wild Cajun girls ventured to Florida due to a slow, boring night in Thibodaux. The beautiful dark-skinned and dark-haired girls laid their towels and chairs adjacent to the volleyball court and celebrated after every point by doing flips, back handsprings, and building an occasional hot-girl pyramid. The guys were digging the girls' beauty, athleticism, and crazy Cajun accents. The girls were digging the fit bodies and cute faces of the Hammerhead Gang. This was a match made in paradise.

There was one ever so slight hitch in the plan. The boys reeked of a combination of dead fish and foul body odor. As it turns out, the Gang had pulled an all-nighter shark fishing, catching an eight-foot Hammerhead and a seven-foot Bull Shark. The boys went straight from shark fishing to the volleyball court. The smell of bloody northern mackerel, bonito, sharks, and perspiration did not blend very well. It was bad. *Really* bad.

Now it was decision time. Could they rinse off in the salty Gulf water enough where the beautiful Cajun girls could endure an evening with them? This was doubtful. Or, could they go home, shower, and come back? The boys all knew if they made the thirty-five-minute drive home to Milton, Florida, that they more than likely would be too exhausted to drive back. Besides, the boys barely had enough gas money to make one trip to the beach, much less two trips. This was a real dilemma and both options sucked.

The boys got in the car and were steadily bickering over what they should do. In the past, they had tried both methods with out-of-town female beach group encounters and failed miserably.

Creigh, staring out the window, said in a soft sobering voice, "I can take care of this."

Danny was puzzled but curious. He looked at Creigh bizarrely and said, "That doesn't sound like the voice of confidence, Creigh."

"Just tell the girls we will meet them in an hour at the disco in the Navarre Beach Pavilion," said Creigh.

None of the boys knew that Creigh had a key to the most luxurious Villa on Navarre Beach. He purposely had not told them. For sure, Danny and John-Boy would have taken up residency in the off season if they knew about this place.

As Nicholas slowly drove them to the mansion, Creigh explained how he got the keys and that this would be a "one-time-thing." The boys would use the shower on the first floor and would leave the place just as they found it. In and out in fifteen minutes. Creigh must have repeated it a dozen times—this is a "one-time-thing."

As they reached their destination, Creigh could see that there were no cars in the driveway, no sandals scattered near the front door, and no towels hanging over the balcony rails. The house was presumed empty. Creigh was nervous and well out of his comfort zone. If caught, this escapade would certainly end his relationship with Sydney and her family.

The Gang took turns using the shower. Things were going smoothly. The boys were steadily getting ready only to appease Creigh but laughing and joking all during the process. Creigh was uncharacteristically but visibly nervous and waited to shower last. As he hurried to dry off and change into a fresh set of clothes, he noticed that John-Boy and Danny were missing. *Surely, they would not try to venture into the main living quarters,* he thought. Creigh quickly glanced around the downstairs area and did not see them. He looked outside, front and back, and still did not see them. By now, he was in panic mode. He ran up the steps to the second floor and shook the locked doorknob. He scampered up to the third floor and found the same situation. Surely, the doors were locked prior to their arrival and Danny and John-Boy were not inside making themselves at home. Creigh had some awful thoughts going through his mind. This was a horrible idea. This "one-time-thing" was certainly going to end his relationship with Sydney, and her parents would certainly tell his parents. They might even call the police and press charges. Creigh was not sure which would be worse.

'Bout that time, he heard some whistling and catcalling coming from the observation deck above the third floor. He dashed up the steps and there he found John-Boy and Danny using the high-powered telescopes to view girls on the beach. Danny was yelling and motioning for a couple of gals to come on up.

Creigh was steaming and did not give either of his buddies a chance to explain themselves. He charged into both boys like an angry bull, knocking both derelicts to the wooden observation deck. John-Boy and Danny had never seen Creigh so angry.

"This is a one-time-thing and you two are going to get us caught!!" exclaimed Creigh. "Get your asses down the steps and go sit in the car!"

By then, the other boys heard the commotion and were standing in front of the house, watching their friends scamper down three flights of steps. Creigh made a quick tour through the first floor to ensure everything was left as they found it. He refolded the towels and returned them to the bathroom closet. Hopefully, they would dry-out before the owners came to visit. He picked up a couple of drink bottles and candy wrappers that the other boys had left and thought, *This is definitely a one-time-thing. I will never allow this to happen again.*

As Creigh was locking the deadbolt, he could hear some laughing, giggling, and unfamiliar voices. He imagined Sydney and her family pulling up in the driveway and looking at his friends in disbelief. He considered running the other direction and letting the boys fend for themselves, denying that he was ever there. *Surely, it is not Sydney's family,* he thought. He peeked around the corner to see two beautiful girls with long blond hair. They were both slightly older than the boys and looked to be in their mid-to-upper twenties. Creigh did not care. He was still angry at Danny and John-Boy for venturing upstairs after he had made it quite clear that this was a "one-time-thing" and to stay on the bottom floor.

Creigh was about to tell the girls that they were on private property, and it would be best for them to leave immediately when one of them stuck out her hand, smiled and said, "Hi, I'm Karen."

Creigh's eyes met Karen's eyes and suddenly his rage melted. He couldn't seem to find the words he was going to use to tell the girls they were trespassing. Nor could he remember the speech he was going to have with the boys about leaving trash on the first floor and disobeying his order to remain on the first floor.

"Well, hello. I'm Creigh."

"What a cool name, Creigh," said Karen.

Creigh could not stop looking at Karen. She had beautiful green eyes, a beautiful face, and a perfectly shaped hourglass body. Her bikini was tiny—which was good in Creigh's eyes. Their handshake lasted about ten seconds. Creigh did not want to let go. Neither did Karen.

"What are y'all doing here?" Creigh asked.

"Your buddies were yelling at us from on top the house, so we decided to venture up to see what was going on," she said. "You have a gorgeous home, Creigh."

Before reasoning, Creigh said, "Thank you."

All the boys looked at Creigh in total disbelief. Creigh would not dare make eye contact with any of them. Besides, he was still staring at Karen. Creigh was brought up to have exceptional manners, but he was so entranced with Karen's beauty that he never introduced himself to Karen's friend, Lisa.

"Can you meet us at the Navarre Pavilion later?" Creigh asked eagerly.

"If you're lucky," said Karen, smiling flirtatiously.

Creigh did not know where she was from, where she went to school, nor if she was single, but he did not care. She was the most beautiful woman he had ever laid eyes on.

The girls turned and walked down the sea oat lined path to the beach. Their family's cottage was much smaller but only three doors down from Creigh's "new home." The boys could not stop gawking at Karen and Lisa as they walked down the beach.

The Hammerheads hastily loaded up in the old Land Shark and headed to the Pavilion. On the ride there, the music was cranked, and all the boys were playing air guitars—even Creigh, who was driving.

Creigh leaned into the back seat and shot a stern look at John-Boy and Danny. Then he smiled and winked as if to say everything was cool.

The Gang pulled into the parking lot of the Pavilion, passed out a few sticks of chewing gum and headed for the disco.

What a weekend. The boys caught sharks, were kings of the beach in volleyball, and danced the night away with a crazy bunch of Louisiana Coon Ass girls, among others. Creigh was focused on Karen and Karen was focused on Creigh.

Karen was from Memphis, Tennessee, and the daughter of a world-renowned banker. She had graduated in finance from Ole Miss and was the understudy at her father's bank. Her family owned a private jet with a private pilot as well. Karen made good use of this luxury and had traveled to places Creigh had never heard of before. The remainder of the Hammerheads were hooked up with the Cajun beauties and Karen's friend, Lisa. They were having a ball. Unfortunately, and too soon, the lights came on and the Pavilion was shutting down. The girls would have to return to their parents' beach cottages and hope to see the boys later in the summer. If only they had a place to go...

Out of nowhere, Creigh said, "Let's all go to my place."

The girls were all smiles and said, "Let's do it."

The boys were looking at Creigh in utter disbelief. He had made such a big deal about going to the Alabama mansion as being a "one-time-thing" that they were wondering if he had lost his mind. Karen must have him in some kind of trance. Regardless, they were all happy.

Creigh quickly laid down the rules. "You can go on the first floor and the observation deck, but the second and third floor are forbidden."

The newly bonded group attracted several beach comers and

eventually there were about twenty people at Creigh's "new house."

Creigh was nervously looking at the mixed crowd of friends and non-Floridian vacationers. They were laughing, dancing, drinking, and having a blast. He was considering asking them to vacate the premises or moving the party to the beach. *This would certainly make everyone mad, but it was probably the best thing to do,* Creigh thought.

Suddenly, Karen stepped into his frame and his thoughts of running-off the partiers vanished.

"Wanna go for a walk on the beach?" asked Karen while extending her hand.

Creigh was so excited, but so nervous. He was calm, cool, and collected in most circumstances...but not this one. Creigh's thought process was summed up like this:

1. *He was trespassing.*
2. *His friends were becoming rowdier as the night rolled on.*
3. *There were unknown people in his fake house (See Number 1).*
4. *The most beautiful girl he had ever seen was asking him to go for a walk on the beach.*

"Sure," said Creigh. Choice Number 4 obviously trumped the other three.

Creigh and Karen walked hand in hand, down the steps, through the sea oats and onto the beach. During the entire walk to the beach, his buddies were catcalling and yelling inappropriate things at the couple. Creigh and Karen laughed it off and proceeded to an area that was not visible from the beach house and had a beautiful view of the moon and Gulf of Mexico. Karen brought a beach towel and laid it neatly out onto the sand, sat down on the towel, and gently patted the spot on the towel beside her. Creigh nervously sat down but could not stop staring at Karen. Karen was a few years older than Creigh, but this was not a big deal to either of them. Creigh had been with many girls on this beach, but none like Karen. She was smart, successful, and beautiful.

Creigh was about to break the silent nervousness by asking a silly question like, "Do you like the beach?" or "Do you like country music?"

Before he could utter the first silly question, Karen leaned into him and kissed him on the lips. It was a soft, but aggressive, kiss. Lips still locked, Karen pushed forward, forcing Creigh to lay back on the towel. Within moments, their arms and legs were wrapped around each other. Every now and then, they would stop kissing and just look into each other's eyes and smile big. Karen was wearing a very short miniskirt and a halter top that was classy but left nothing to the imagination. Creigh was wearing casual pull-up gym shorts, and it was visibly obvious how much Karen had excited him. The newly formed couple continued to roll around on (and off) the beach towel. Within ten minutes, almost all their clothes had been abandoned.

As much as they wanted to, Creigh and Karen agreed to not have sexual intercourse on their first encounter. The new couple kissed and caressed until the sun was peaking over the eastern horizon. The sound of the waves lapping upon the shore sounded so peaceful. Creigh and Karen shook the sand from their clothes and redressed. Karen looked at Creigh and started giggling. Did he look that funny? Was the bulge in his gym shorts more visible in the daylight?

"Your shirt is on backward and inside out," said Karen.

Creigh laughed and pulled off his shirt and turned it right-side-in.

"I wouldn't have said anything, but I wanted to see that body one more time," said Karen.

They laughed and had one more affectionate hug before Creigh put his shirt back on.

Karen and Creigh wrapped up together in the oversized beach towel and slowly headed back to the beach house. Creigh had been with many girls in the past ten years, but none had made him feel like Karen did. *Hopefully, Karen feels the same way about me,* he thought.

As Creigh and Karen walked up the balcony steps, they could still hear the music. Fortunately, someone had turned it down enough where the neighbors would not call the police. As they navigated their way through the house, Creigh saw several bodies scattered throughout on couches, beds, and the floor. Some were coupled and some were not. Some were clad, some were not.

As it turned out, this was just one of many nights that the boys visited "Creigh's Mansion." The Hammerheads used the place year-round. Creigh's unwritten rule was no one was allowed to be on the premises unless he was present. Unbeknownst to Creigh, all the other boys visited the mansion on occasion, on their own. The boys spent so much time at their new hangout that they renamed it the O-T-T. This was in reference to, and in jest of, Creigh repeatedly telling them that this would be a "one-time-thing."

Boy, was he ever so wrong.

6

SMART BUT NOT THAT SMART

It was a new Saturday night, and the Hammerhead Gang was ready for a new adventure. The boys were headed south on Highway 87 and the destination was once again Navarre Beach. The plan was to meet up with some young, beautiful vacationers. Although in reality, the true hook-up with sex and everything rarely happened. It was really all about the hunt. The hunt was the fun part. In this instance, it was not a Shark Hunt. It was a pretty Southern Belle Hunt. The Hammerhead Gang knew the calendar dates for every holiday and spring break of every college. It was important to know and understand who was present. This week was, among other states, the Louisiana summer break. As the boys knew from previous encounters, Louisiana girls were dark-haired, dark-tanned, very curvy, and loved to party. This was a favorite week of the Hammerhead Gang.

Incidentally, Creigh and Karen stayed in contact on a weekly basis. Despite all the shenanigans with his buddies and the spring breakers, Karen was still top on his list—and she felt the same way about him.

Besides, she was having her own fun, jet-setting around the world in her father's private aircraft.

The boys were all squeezed into Nicholas's Land Shark and listening to a variety of country, rock, and R&B music. The boys could never agree on what music to listen to, so they were constantly changing radio stations. This was the important responsibility of the person in the front passenger seat. Nicholas was a terrible driver so, as usual, Creigh took the wheel and Nicholas was on self-assigned radio duty.

The music was blaring, and the boys were singing to their hearts' content. The Hammerheads had just crossed the Ole Yellow River bridge when suddenly, out of nowhere, a vehicle raced up behind them and was no less than five feet from their rear bumper. Blue lights were now flashing in the rearview mirror. It was obvious that the police officer wanted them to pull over. Creigh eased over into the right-of-way and came to a complete stop. It was very dark, and no other vehicles were present. They were not drinking, they were not speeding, what had they done? Looking in the rearview mirror, Creigh could see the shadow of a large man wearing a cowboy hat and carrying a nightstick flashlight slowly limping toward them. As the law officer neared the back end of Nicholas's car, a loud thump and the subsequent sound of breaking glass or plastic was heard. Had Deputy Delay slipped due to his recently injured knee?

Creigh lowered his window and handed the officer his license. Without speaking, Deputy Delay returned to his cruiser to do whatever law officers do when they return to their car during a traffic stop. The boys all smirked because they recognized Deputy Delay, but he had no clue who they were. It had been a while since the tire escapade and Deputy Delay was still limping. That tumble down the hill must have really hurt.

The boys had been waiting for what seemed like an hour when they heard the thump of Delay's flashlight on the driver's side window. Remarkably, it sounded just like the thump they had heard when Delay was first approaching the back of the car earlier. Creigh lowered the window.

"Turn off the engine and step out of the vehicle," grunted Deputy Delay.

Creigh obliged the Deputy's request. Deputy Delay then hobbled to the rear of the car and motioned for Creigh to follow. The rest of the boys remained in the car and were ready for some night life fun.

"Do you know why I pulled you over, punk?" snapped Deputy Delay.

"No sir, I don't," replied Creigh.

"You have a broken taillight. Can we take a quick look in the trunk to see if there is any wiring damage?" continued Deputy Delay.

This was a bizarre request, but Creigh was brought up to respect his elders and agreed wholeheartedly. It was very dark, and Creigh was anxious. He fiddled around with the keys until he finally inserted the correct key into the trunk latch.

As he raised the trunk lid, Creigh's heart sank. Delay shined his flashlight into the filthy trunk and there it was—the "greed tire" and pull rope, just as Delay had suspected. Nicholas was supposed to remove the greed tire and pull rope prior to this planned adventure but somehow forgot.

What the boys did not know is that early on the night of the greed tire escapade, Delay had stumbled upon their getaway car. Being an experienced cop, he had found this parked car suspicious and had written down the make, model, and license plate number. He even made a note about the unique shark fin hood ornament. In most instances, this is the result of a stolen, abandoned, or a broken-down vehicle. However, after Deputy Delay was yanked down the hill, he knew that the ole Land Shark must have been involved in the getaway. It was the only reasonable explanation why they could not find the perpetrators that night.

Also, a couple of weeks after his "fall" down the hill, Deputy Delay hobbled through the Mulat Swamp and found the island, milk crates, dim trails, and even the raft. He had been relentlessly looking for the vehicle with a shark fin hood ornament for quite some time, and finally hit paydirt.

Creigh sat with his hands cuffed behind his back in the rear seat of the cruiser as Deputy Delay drove off to the north toward Milton. The other boys continued to the south toward Navarre Beach. Their plans were destroyed. Nicholas felt bad about not removing the tire, but they all agreed that it probably would not have mattered. Deputy Delay was a seasoned cop and would have found a way to tie the vehicle to the tire escapade and eventually to the boys. A bigger problem was that their leader, their planner, their "trouble circumventer" was no longer available to come up with a plan. This was unchartered water for the Hammerheads. Creigh had always made the decisions and kept them on point. What should they do? One thing for sure, they all agreed that Deputy Delay was now added to the Shark List.

The roadside was quiet, dark, and somewhat eerie. Deputy Delay sat on the hood of his car, smoking a big stogie, and relishing his victory. One of the punks who had pulled him down the hill that fateful night was in the backseat of his cruiser. His long-term plan was to arrest each of these boys, one by one, and make them pay for his injuries and embarrassment. In a roundabout way, they were on *his* Shark List.

Creigh was uncertain why Delay pulled over on the roadside right-of-way again but decided to play the only card he had available. He tapped on the cruiser backseat passenger window and Deputy Delay slowly hobbled over and glared at him. As a lead in, Creigh humbly apologized to Deputy Delay, explaining that they would never intentionally target a law officer nor old people.

Creigh then asked, "Do you know Nicholas's dad, Sergeant Kelly, with the City Police Department?"

Deputy Delay smiled and said, "Yes, Colie Kelly and I go way back."

Creigh did all he could to keep from grinning because he knew this was his big break. Deputy Delay told Creigh about him and Sergeant Kelly working together on the federal drug task force team and busting some serious drug dealers several years back. Deputy Delay spoke of them taking several training classes together over the past twenty-five years. He boasted of what a great cop Colie was, even if he did work for the city versus the county.

Deputy Delay was softening up. He finally smiled and opened the rear passenger door.

"Step out of the car, young man," said Deputy Delay.

Creigh's plan had worked. He had actually talked the meanest old grumpy cop in the Florida panhandle to release him.

While reaching for his handcuff keys, Deputy Delay politely asked Creigh to turn around.

Creigh was beside himself and immediately turned around and presented his hands to Delay making the uncuffing easier.

In a nanosecond, Creigh found himself lying face-down on the roadside with the most excruciating pain imaginable going through his right shoulder. He raised his head and glanced over just in time for that same flashlight to crease the skin just above his left eye.

That was the last he remembered until he was being dragged from the cruiser at the Sheriff's Office. His body ached from head-to-toe. His face was covered in blood, and he was still in handcuffs. He had obviously taken a severe beating from Deputy Delay.

"Don't you ever try to escape again!" Delay shouted for everyone to hear.

Creigh did not know what to think at this point. His plan had failed...miserably.

7

SOUTHERN JUSTICE

Creigh laid on the cold floor of Cell 17 in the Santa Rosa County Jail. He had been fingerprinted, photographed, and questioned. He laid exhausted, bloodied, and bruised. There were constant interruptions, arguing and fighting within his cell block. It felt like a bad dream. Whether it was sleep or unconsciousness from his injuries, he finally closed his eyes and dozed off. What was the next step? Were his friends trying to get him out? Did his parents know?

Creigh awoke to a sharp pain in the middle of his forehead. Two extremely large Black men were standing over him. They both were wearing smelly wife-beater T-shirts and most of their visible skin was covered with tattoos. Creigh assumed correctly that one of them had thumped him in the forehead with his index finger, which was the size of a large carrot. It was Ray-T and Buckles. Buckles had spent several years in prison for beating a man with his belt buckle, hence the nickname. Ray-T was much bigger than Buckles, which is impressive since Buckles is every bit of 6'4" and 250 pounds. Both men were at least ten years older than Creigh. He only knew who they were due to their violent reputation in the little town of Milton, Florida.

"Get up, punk," said Buckles.

This was the second time he had been called "punk" in twenty-four hours. He wondered if he was about to receive the same wrath he received the last time he was addressed as such.

Creigh slowly stood up. He held back a grunt, although he was in severe pain. He did not want his unwelcome foes to see any sign of weakness even though he was hurting so bad he could barely stand up. Creigh was a very healthy young man, but he was clearly outmatched by these fellas. There was a total of ten men in Cell 17. Most of them ignored what was going on because they did not want to be hurt or further punished. After all, they were all *innocent*. Sarcasm intended.

As the two men inched closer to Creigh, they were shouting vulgar language at him about his momma and sister. Creigh was hastily calculating a plan. Creigh was a negotiator and had avoided physical conflict most of his life. He couldn't talk his way out this time—he was going to have to fight. If he did nothing, they both would pulverize him. If he sucker-punched one of them, he might knock him out and then only have to grapple with one man that was twice his size and ten times as experienced at fighting.

Ray-T and Buckles were now within striking distance. Ray-T grabbed Creigh's collar. Creigh ripped away from Ray-T and, at the same time, used his momentum to land a solid punch on Buckles. It was a direct hit to his jawbone. Buckles fell to the floor like a mighty oak tree crashing in the forest.

But as expected, Ray-T punched Creigh before he could defend himself. The first punch landed on Creigh's left shoulder...the same shoulder Deputy Delay had pulverized with his flashlight. The second punch hit him square in the nose. The back of Creigh's head hit the cell wall as blood began gushing from both his nostrils. Creigh was in trouble. He was weak and weary as he stumbled away from his attacker. Creigh landed helplessly on the floor and was unable to protect himself. Ray-T was now standing over Creigh, contemplating whether to kick, punch, or strangle him.

Creigh closed his eyes and started reevaluating how much fun they had had with the greed tire. His mind was everywhere—*how could he have handled his encounter with Deputy Delay better? Why didn't he make sure the tire and rope were removed? Should he have tried to negotiate with Ray-T and Buckles first?* All of this went through his head in a split second.

Just as Ray-T was about to end Creigh's life, a flurry of punches and kicks erupted in front of Creigh. Creigh did not feel a thing. Was he so numb from his other injuries that he lost all sense of feeling? Was he already unconscious? Creigh cracked open one of his eyes.

To his delight, both Ray-T and Buckles were lying on the floor beside him, unconscious. A short but extremely muscular Black man stood over Buckles and Ray-T. He glanced over at Creigh while maintaining a fighting posture, waiting for either of the big men to make a move.

Creigh was still trying to figure out if this was real or an after-death experience.

"IGYB Forever, Creigh," said the soft-spoken hero.

Creigh knew exactly what this meant and exactly who this was. IGYB Forever was short for "I Got Your Back Forever."

Creigh struggled to open his other eye and could see that it was exactly who he thought it was—Willy McClain, a childhood friend. His very best childhood friend.

Legend has it, Willy was the best running back to never play high school football in the state of Florida. He was the owner of every Pee-Wee football record. The Hammerheads were excellent athletes, but Willy McClain was in a league of his own. Willy was stronger and faster than all the other boys. Creigh and Willy had played together often as kids. Creigh even had a picture of both of them taped to his bedroom mirror; arm-n-arm, raising their index fingers after winning a youth championship. Creigh and Willy had made a pact back then that even though they were of a different race and clearly raised in different settings that they would always stand up for each other. Hence the slogan "IGYB Forever."

By the tenth grade, Willy's father had been murdered; and his mother, who was addicted to crack cocaine, moved to an unknown location up north. Willy lived on the streets and, for obvious reasons, found it hard making it to school—much less football practice. As a result, the old southern style high school coaches proudly dismissed Willy from the team. He eventually dropped out of school and took to a life of crime. Sadly, Willy was a product of the system. This was a common theme in the south. There was no doubt in Creigh's mind that Willy would have played professional football if someone had only taken pity on him, picked him up for practice, and helped him with his schoolwork.

Over the years, Creigh had quietly kept up with Willy's life and had vowed to do something about it. Like most people, he never took the next step to help Willy. He had not held up his end of "IGYB Forever." His childhood friend had literally just saved his life for no other reason except that he kept their vow.

"IGYB Forever, Willy," whispered Creigh.

The jail house deputies eventually showed up and unlocked Cell 17. It was fairly evident which parties were involved in the Cell 17 brawl. Willy and Creigh were uneventfully handcuffed and escorted out of Cell 17. Ray-T and Buckles remained on the floor, and it looked as if both would require medical attention. Creigh and Willy did not even get a chance to talk. The guards took Willy up a flight of stairs to Cell 25. Prior to locking him in the isolation cell, they made sure he knew who was in charge.

By now, Ray-T and Buckles were awake and creating a disturbance that could be heard throughout the entire concrete block building. Their loud and belligerent behavior was contagious. Soon there was yelling and screaming from every cell. As Creigh was being escorted past Cell 25, he could see Willy laying on the cold floor. Willy's face looked bruised, and he had a trickle of blood running from his nose.

"I am going to come find you and help you...I promise," said Creigh.

Willy gave him a strong and powerful look and said, "Don't worry about me, I am just fine."

Willy maintained his pride even though he had just been man-handled by a couple of jailhouse deputies. Creigh felt horrible. He had abandoned his childhood friend for years only to be saved by him at his most vulnerable time in life. Willy did not have to help him... but he did. Willy would probably face additional charges for his role in the fight in Cell 17...but he had defended Creigh anyway. Worse, Willy would undoubtedly have to face Ray-T and Buckles again at some point, but he chose to help his childhood friend. IGYB Forever...

Creigh was escorted up to the prisoner release desk. Seeing the sign that read "Prisoner Release Desk" made him feel so dirty, but at the same time made him feel relieved. His handcuffs were removed, and an icepack was provided for his bleeding nose. Sheriff Hyde Powers emerged and gave him a quick wink and smile. The last time someone in uniform acted nice to him, he ended up with a compelling pain in his left shoulder subsequently followed by unconsciousness. Creigh was cautious to smile, move, or do anything that might cause an adverse reaction. Sheriff Powers was a wall of a man—what some would call "Country Big." It seemed like everyone associated with the

County Jail was aberrantly big and overly mean. Sheriff Powers was a lifetime resident of Santa Rosa County and, more importantly, an avid football fan.

"Are you all right, son?" Sheriff Powers asked.

Creigh was not sure if he should lie and say he was fine or tell the Sheriff how horrible Deputy Delay had treated him. Creigh quickly reasoned that the Sheriff already knew what had happened and that his best option was to just say he was ok.

Before he could nod his head yes, Sheriff Powers grabbed Creigh by the collar, walked him down a hall into a stairwell corridor. He pinned Creigh to the wall where, conveniently, no one could see them. Creigh could not take another beating.

"Listen very closely, son," whispered Sheriff Powers.

His face was less than two inches from Creigh's face and his breath smelled like cheap chewing tobacco. His eyes would put the fear of God in the strongest of men.

"All of this has been removed from the official records but will officially remain in the unofficial records. Do you understand what I am saying?" asked Sheriff Powers.

Before Creigh could answer, Sheriff Powers inched closer. By now, he was holding Creigh by the throat and Creigh could hardly breathe. With every word he spoke, he spit a mouthful of nasty, brown tobacco slobber onto Creigh's face. The one positive was that he did not have to worry about swallowing the nasty stuff because of the bear-claw grip the Sheriff had on his throat.

"If I ever hear of you causing any trouble in this county again, I will come find you and you will wish to God that you were still in the hands of Deputy Delay. Do you understand me?"

Sheriff Powers's face was scarred-over multiple times. Creigh could not imagine the many battles this man had fought and won over the past thirty years.

Creigh whimpered out, "Yes, sir."

Sheriff Powers clinched Creigh's throat a little tighter one more time just to let him know who was in charge.

After a few more seconds, Sheriff Powers simultaneously backed away and loosened his grip on Creigh's throat.

Creigh had been taught all his life to respect his elders, yet he just had physical confrontations with four adults, all on the same day! As Creigh cautiously walked toward the County Jail exit, he could feel Sheriff Powers glaring at him.

Just before he pushed the door open, Sheriff Powers very sternly yelled, "Creigh!"

Creigh turned and sheepishly said, "Yes, sir?"

In the back of his mind, he was wondering if the Sheriff had changed his mind and was going to toss him back in Cell 17. Or worse, give him his own dose of punishment.

"Congratulations on the state championships. You guys made our community proud. Good luck to you!" yelled Sheriff Powers.

Creigh nodded his head and continued to the exit. There was never a record of Creigh being in jail, much less in the back of a police car. There was never a record of a fight in Cell 17 on that fateful night. Ray-T, Buckles, and Willy remained in jail for several weeks. Eventually, all three pleaded out on time served.

Creigh had just experienced "southern justice" at its finest.

8

SUMMERTIME FUN

Unlike spring break and early summer break, it was late summertime and tourist season was in full swing. The Hammerhead Gang decided to venture out to Destin for the weekend. Creigh was still healing from his physical and mental wounds and was ready for some fun. The boys planned to crash at a cheap hotel but go play at one of the expensive resorts as if they were staying there.

Using their fake car pass, they slipped right pass the security guards and on to the sprawling resort property. The resort pool was their destination. The white sandy beaches and sparkling green water were beautiful, but the pool was where the mostly younger crowd hung out. There would be a live band, friendly people, and most important, beautiful girls everywhere. The boys snagged a couple of lounge chairs strategically located between the pool and the band. The crowd was mainly college students and young professionals. There was also a small mixture of families and a few snowbirds who decided to stick it out. Most of the single crowd was a few years older than the Hammerhead

Gang, but due to their dedicated gym ethics, the boys fit right in physically. Within seconds, the T-shirts were removed, revealing their chiseled bodies, and the boys were standing waist-deep in the pool.

It did not take long for the Gang to make friends. Several girls from Arkansas had marked their territory with beach chairs, towels, and oversized beach bags. The young boys gave it a try but were no match for these seasoned girls. They were mid-thirties divorcées and identified the youth of the Hammerhead Gang right away.

A newly married young couple, Kent and Kimberly Poole, were seated next to the guys and were quite amused at the Hammerhead Gang's effort to impress the Arkansas ladies. After all, Kent and Kimberly had met five years earlier at this same location. Kimberly Poole was a beautiful young southern girl who had made a name for herself over the years by winning bikini contests up and down the Gulf Coast. She was not the brightest bulb on the tree but was sweet, kind, and had an amazing body. Kent was a new partner in a large law firm in Jackson, Mississippi. Kent's family was loaded with money. They were one of the largest landowners in the Southeast United States and owned several sawmills. Truth be known, his family status had much more to do with landing a beautiful girl like Kimberly and becoming a partner in the prestigious Jackson law firm. Since they had not yet started a family, Kent and Kimberly traveled the world. Just this year alone, Kimberly boasted that they had visited Park City, Cabo, and Briancon, France. The boys smiled and acted impressed. Actually, this meant nothing to the boys—they were not familiar with any of those places!

After watching the Hammerhead Gang's dismal efforts at trying to impress the older Arkansas girls, Kent called them over for a pep talk.

"You guys are obviously younger than these girls and your only chance is to make them believe you are rich...extremely rich," said Kent.

The boys were intrigued. They enjoyed the company of Kent and

Kimberly all day and now Kent was going to show them the ropes.

"Drop a hint to the girls that Danny's father won the largest lottery jackpot in Florida history and owns the resort," Kent Poole told them in a whispering tone.

Nicholas piped in, "But that would be a lie."

The other boys looked at him in disbelief and gave him a cumulative, "Duh."

Despite resistance from Nicholas, the guys fine-tuned Kent's plan. Creigh would tell them that Danny's lottery-winning father owned the resort, but Danny was modest and would not talk about it.

Creigh delivered the punch line and in no time, the Arkansas gals were dancing with the boys, song after song. Kent and Kimberly pulled their chairs over and partied with the Hammerhead Gang and their new girlfriends the remainder of the day.

Creigh knew all the band members. The legendary Ike, Mike, Tim, and Shannon were the most famous and popular band on the Gulf Coast. Creigh let them in on the lottery joke as well. During one of the band breaks, Ike announced over the microphone that Danny, "the heir to the largest Florida lottery jackpot in history" was in the house.

By the end of the day, the Arkansas girls had a lot of competition and all the boys, except John-Boy, had each exchanged phone numbers with at least three girls.

John-Boy had made eye contact with the extremely sexy, heavily tattooed, guest singer of the band the minute they arrived. Every time "Sunflower" would make her way to the stage, John-Boy would stand on the dance floor, directly in front of her and slowly sway dance. The songs she was singing were much faster-paced. He was completely out of rhythm. This was mostly likely due to the influence of the drugs he had taken, but he didn't care what anyone thought. Sometimes he would sway dance with this cute little blond preschooler, which made everyone laugh hysterically.

After each set, John-Boy and Sunflower would disappear, only to reappear with glassy eyes, untucked clothing, and messed up hair. John-Boy was the only Hammerhead that openly smoked pot and occasionally did other recreational drugs. The other boys did not appreciate his drug habit, but they tolerated it.

As the sun was setting, the band had left, and the crowd was thinning out. Kent Poole had just finished drinking his sixth Smoked Old Fashioned of the day. The boys thought this was a really cool drink and vowed to drink one on their next outing.

Kent Poole made one last "smoke and pee" break. When he returned, he informed Kimberly it was time for them to pack-up their beach gear and hit the road. This was their last day of vacation and they had already checked out of the hotel.

The Pooles had a six-hour drive home to Jackson, Mississippi and would struggle to make it to work the next morning. The Hammerhead Gang thanked Kent for his dating advice, shook hands, hugged necks, and wished them a safe trip home.

The Arkansas girls had to leave as well and informed the boys they would be back again soon. The boys jumped in the ole Land Shark and headed back to their low budget hotel. It was certainly not befitting for the largest Florida jackpot lottery winner. Regardless, they showered and then hit a couple of the local nightclubs on Highway 98.

At 3 a.m., Creigh could barely keep his eyes open and was pleading with the Gang to return to the hotel. After a quick stop for some grits and eggs at a 24-hour breakfast joint, the guys finally made it back to the hotel for some sleep. John-Boy was nowhere to be found, which was not unusual. The next morning, they briefly looked for John-Boy and collectively decided to leave him. They felt certain John-Boy was in good hands with Sunflower. What a fun weekend for all!

9

LITTLE EMMA

The five-year-old girl laid lifeless in the corner, behind the toilet in the locked handicap stall of the men's restroom. Her curly blond hair was soaked in blood and her petite lime green bathing suit top was lying on the floor beside her. Emma's bathing suit bottom was missing. It was clear that she had been brutally raped, beaten, and strangled. It was hours before a resort custodial employee found her. Immediately the janitor became the prime suspect. After all, he had a police record and was currently on probation. The police focused on the custodial worker and spent an enormous amount of critical time questioning him. Eventually, he was cleared, which left no other suspects.

Creigh didn't learn about the rape and beating of little Emma at the Destin resort until the next day. It was on every radio and TV station. Her family was vacationing from Birmingham, Alabama, and their lives would be changed forever. Creigh, for some strange reason, felt responsible for what had happened. Little Emma had been killed on his watch. He was there, less than one hundred feet away. Surely, he could have picked out the predator prior to the attack. Creigh remembered seeing little Emma splashing around in the shallow end of the pool, smiling and laughing in her lime green bathing suit. As little kids do, she was in her own little paradise. Had he been paying too much attention to the Arkansas girls and not enough to what was going on around him? Creigh was secretly a very emotional person. He cried privately in his bedroom for almost an hour before calling Nicholas, Danny, and Terrance to tell them what had happened. John-Boy was still nowhere to be found.

The boys met at the gym for their daily workout. The death of little Emma put everything into a different perspective. Their fun weekend did not seem so fun now. John-Boy did not show up for their workout, but again, this was not unusual for him.

Later that evening, the boys were hanging out at the Milton City Park basketball courts and trying to replay their day to determine who could have possibly been the child rapist at the Destin resort.

Finally, Danny said what was on everyone else's mind, "What about John-Boy?"

There was an angry and sinking feeling among the Hammerheads. In the back of each one's mind, there was a thought that somehow John-Boy might just be involved with the death of little Emma. Immediately, the boys were convicting John-Boy just as the police had convicted the poor, black Destin resort janitor. Surely one of their own could not do something as monstrous as this. John-Boy was certainly different and would have some hard questions to answer—where did he and Sunflower go every forty-five minutes? Why did he disappear at the end of the night? Where was he now? Was she the same little preschooler he was dancing with on the dance floor?

The next day, Creigh spoke with John-Boy's brother, who said John-Boy arrived home at about 4 a.m. and was still in bed. Creigh gathered up the Gang and headed to John-Boy's house. As usual, the front door to his house was unlocked and the Hammerheads walked straight back to his bedroom. His room was beyond filthy, as was the remainder of the house. John-Boy was abruptly awakened by his best buddies. He cracked a smile and asked if they had scored as he did. The boys were not interested in his sexual encounter with Sunflower. They wanted to know why he had murdered little Emma.

"We need to talk to you. Get dressed," said Creigh.

Although he did not like being bossed, John-Boy knew it was something serious and threw some clothes on that had been lying on the floor, put on a pair of sunglasses, and squeezed into the Land Shark. He smelled like a cross between stale marijuana, whiskey, and bad body odor. It was awful and everyone stared at him in disgust, but he couldn't care less.

The boys drove north on Highway 87 for about ten miles outside of Milton, Florida before turning-off on Highway 182 and eventually onto a dirt road in the Chumuckla community. The ride was eerily quiet. What would the Hammerheads do if John-Boy confessed to the brutal murder? Nicholas pulled over in a spot where they normally parked their vehicle during hunting season.

The boys all got out. John-Boy had all kinds of thoughts going through his head. *Do the other Hammerheads want to try some pot? Cool! Are they going to confess to being gay? Not cool! After all, I was the only one that hooked up this weekend.*

"Where did you and Sunflower go during her singing breaks?" asked Creigh.

"Why does it matter to you?" rebutted John-Boy.

Creigh was shaking. John-Boy had this smart-alecky grin on his face that made matters worse. Before Creigh could repeat his question, Nicholas stepped in front of Creigh, pounced on the much weaker

John-Boy and had him pinned to the trunk of the car.

All the boys were yelling in some form or another, "Why did you do this!?" "She was just an innocent child!!" "What is wrong with you!?"

John-Boy sobered up quickly. He was stunned. "What the frick are y'all talking about?"

Creigh was quickly relieved when he heard that question from John-Boy. He had known John-Boy since they were the same age as little Emma and he could tell by the tone that John-Boy was unaware of the murder.

It took Creigh, Terrance, and Danny to peel Nicholas off John-Boy, who was still confused. Creigh quickly told John-Boy about the bathroom murder of little Emma. John-Boy was angry at his so-called friends but seemed unfazed by the story. He had been through a lot in his young life, including alleged abuse from his uncle at a very young age. This was an emotional moment for the entire Gang. They were relieved that the murderer was not John-Boy but upset that the child rapist and killer had not been found.

After apologizing, chest bumping, and awkwardly hugging John-Boy, the Hammerheads climbed back into the car and headed back to town. Their friend was not a murderer, but who was? In a funny inquisitive way, Creigh asked, "Where did you and the sexy tattooed woman go during her singing breaks?"

John-Boy, anxious to tell everyone about his sexual encounter, smiled and said, "We found a cozy but filthy little janitor closet with a cot. It was small, but air conditioned and served its purpose."

Creigh, now jumping on the custodial worker bandwagon, anxiously asked, "Did you ever see the janitor?"

"Nah, we didn't," replied John-Boy.

"Your new friend from Jackson, Mississippi poked his head in the door, thinking it might be a locker room. Looked like he was trying to locate a place to change-out his daughter's bathing suit," said John-Boy.

Nicholas slammed on brakes and pulled over on the side of the road. John-Boy thought he was in for another attack from his friends.

"What did you say?" said Creigh.

"I said the guy, I believe his name was Kent, walked in on me and Sunflower. It was dark but we could see him due to the light behind him. His timing could not have been worse. We were in-the-short-rows if you know what I mean, and did not care for the distraction. He had his daughter with him, the cute little girl in the lime green bathing suit—the one I danced with on the dance floor. He apologized to us and backed out."

The boys all knew that Kent and Kimberly did not have children. All the Hammerhead Gang but John-Boy were fairly certain now that Kent Poole was the killer. The Gang brought John-Boy up to speed and as usual, he showed little emotion. What do they do now? Should they call the authorities? Should they tell their parents? Little Emma deserved swift and severe justice.

The boys agreed that they needed to undoubtedly involve the police. The question was: when should they involve the police?

Even though they would go to the authorities and, as ridiculous as it sounded, Kent Poole was now on the Shark List. He was in a completely different category than all the other Shark Listers.

Again, the Hammerheads were in unchartered waters. Kent would have to pay for his crime...pay dearly. As usual, Creigh and Terrance wanted to take the high road and call the police immediately. Nicholas and Danny wanted to execute him in a painful manner and John-Boy had no opinion. Creigh really could not believe they were even talking about putting Kent Poole on the Shark List. It certainly appeared odd to have a murderer on the list right below Miss Ida and Mr. Gurkey.

10

THE INVESTIGATION
OF KENT POOLE

It had been a few months since Creigh's jail house experience and only a few days since the murder of little Emma. The boys had not come forward to authorities with the information on Kent and Kimberly Poole, only because they were trying to find out more information. Creigh and Danny spent countless hours researching the background on Kent and Kimberly Poole. They tried to recall every conversation with the couple, looking for hints, clues, or evidence. Most of the information they found was about how much money and land they had. The Poole family were not millionaires—they were billionaires. They were quietly one of the richest families in the United States.

On a whim, Creigh searched through public records for "recent unsolved child murders." What he found would change everything. There were hundreds of missing children cases in the United States and there were twenty-six unsolved child rape/murder cases this year alone on the books. Of the twenty-six cases, eighteen were inner city murders of African American children. Of the remaining eight cases, one was in Destin; one was in Park City, Utah; and one was in Jackson, Mississippi—all three cases occurred at the same time and same place that Kent Poole was present! Creigh expanded his research to include Briancon, France, and sure enough, there was an unsolved child murder/rape case from earlier this year. This now made four unsolved female child murder cases that occurred while Kent Poole just so happened to be in the same town. Coincidence? No way.

The boys were furious and anxious. They now were 99 percent sure that Kent was a serial child rapist and murderer. How did they not see it while in Destin? Was Kimberly involved? Were there other cases as well?

Further investigation of Kent Poole revealed that four years ago, he had spent six months in jail for tax evasion. Kent had not paid taxes on $230,000 in income. The public records showed that the Pooles owned several hundred thousand acres of timber land. The records indicated that the family was suspected of growing and distributing drugs throughout the United States. Allegedly, there was a million dollars in hidden drug dealing income, but the IRS could only account for $230,000 in unreported timber wages. There were rumors that the money was in overseas bank accounts or buried on one of their vast properties. Kent Poole was not the nice gentleman that the boys thought he was. Kent was a billionaire, drug dealer, child rapist, and murderer. He was a serial killer. He had to be stopped...

11

THE RETURN OF
DEPUTY DELAY

Creigh and Danny left the public library after midnight, totally exhausted from searching public records. They had enough information to come forward and have Kent Poole arrested. Creigh wondered if Kent had other relatives that knew of, or participated in, these horrific crimes. He wondered how many years this had been going on. Kent not only murdered and raped children, but he also left them on display for others to find. In addition, in each case, the child's panties or bathing suit bottom was missing—an indication that he was keeping a trophy for his kill. This was a very sick person.

Creigh made a left turn onto Old Chumuckla Highway and noticed a car almost joined to his rear bumper. After further examination from both boys, they could see that it was a police cruiser.

Creigh pondered, *Was I speeding? I don't think so...Did I run a red light? No. Did I use my turn signal?* About that time the blue lights came on. *Oh no, not again,* thought Creigh.

Creigh's only choice was to turn down a dim country dirt road. Old

Chumuckla Highway's right-of-way was unsafe for stopped vehicles. As his car came to a stop, Creigh could see a large man with a cowboy hat sitting in the driver's seat of the patrol car.

The deputy, presumably Deputy Delay, sat in his patrol car for a solid ten minutes. Creigh and Danny were fairly certain they had done nothing wrong but were unsure of what was about to happen. The blue lights continue to flash, and all Creigh could think of was the brutal beating he had endured a few months back.

Should we jump out of the car and run? Could we "handle" Deputy Delay? Or better yet, should we drive as fast as we can to the police station?

Their hearts were pounding in rhythm with the blue lights. Both boys had a very sick feeling and could barely speak. About that time, the driver's side door to the patrol car opened. The boys were looking through the rearview mirrors and could see the shadow of Deputy Delay slowly walking, still with a slight limp from his knee injury, toward their vehicle with the infamous flashlight in his hand. He looked to be seven feet tall, and his gun was visibly strapped to his side.

"Handling" Deputy Delay was suddenly not an option.

All the windows in Creigh's car were fogged due to their heavy breathing. Creigh cracked his window open just enough to peek out and visibly see Deputy Delay. He did not want to spare enough room in the window opening for the Deputy to strike him with his flashlight.

"Let me see your license," he said, as if he did not know who Creigh was.

Creigh slid his license through the cracked window. Delay stared at it for what seemed like five minutes, never looking up at the boys.

Finally, Office Delay bent down to the level of the cracked window. The boys could see his terrifying bloodshot eyes. He was old but not frail. His skin looked like leather and was heavily scarred. His nose was spread out over a good four inches of his face. *Probably got that way from countless fights with perps*, Creigh thought.

Deputy Delay slipped the driver's license into the front pocket of his freshly starched shirt and stepped back about two feet from the car. His feet were slightly spread in an athletic postured position, and his right hand was on his gun.

"Step out of the car, please."

The long-handled flashlight was shining directly in Creigh's eyes, disabling him from clearly seeing Deputy Delay. A million things were racing through Creigh's head. *Am I about to receive another beating? Am I going to jail? I wonder if I will be reunited with Buckles and Ray-T again?*

"You, on the passenger side, get out as well." This was unusual for an officer to allow both men out of the car at the same time. The young men complied.

Deputy Delay took a few steps backward, glaring at both boys then turned toward his cruiser and muttered, "Follow me."

He used his flashlight to guide himself to the back side of the patrol car. Delay had left himself wide open for the boys to attack him. This seemed odd for such a seasoned officer.

As the boys cautiously approached the back of the patrol car, Danny whispered to Creigh, "He is positioning us away from the camera of his patrol car."

Creigh and Danny now feared for their lives. This was so atypical of any police encounter they had seen on TV or read about. The boys stood side-by-side with their butts to the patrol car. Deputy Delay now looked to be about eight feet tall and was standing a mere foot away. Was this how their lives would end?

The greed tire—what a stupid, stupid, stupid idea, Creigh thought.

Deputy Delay removed his hat and placed it on the trunk of the patrol car beside his flashlight. His arms were hanging down and his hands were slightly clasped, resting on his enormous belly. He looked kinda sad and remorseful. The boys were certainly unsure of what was going on.

"You boys humiliated me a few months back."

There were about thirty seconds of silence with both boys staring at the ground.

"I have done quite a bit of research on you and your crew. I know all about the Hammerhead Gang and the Shark List."

There was about thirty more seconds of silence with both boys staring at the ground.

Deputy Delay inched closer. "I pulled you over because I want you to know that my nephew is Billy Davidson."

The boys gave an awkward look to each other because they were not familiar with Billy Davidson. Maybe there was a misunderstanding and Delay was confused.

"Booger Boy Billy," said Delay.

The boys acknowledged Delay by nodding their heads.

"A female drug informant told me you bought a bag of marijuana from her a long time ago," said Delay. "It was back when you were in high school."

The boys hesitated but reluctantly acknowledged Delay again by nodding their heads.

"The bag was marked, and when we found it in Dusty Middlebrook's locker, we knew what had happened. We were going to bust you guys, but Billy told me that you guys were always nice to him and told him that you would never let Dusty harm him again. I put two and two together and realized you were standing-up for my nephew."

The boys did not know what to say. Deputy Delay's investigation could have not been more correct.

"Billy is a special needs child and will always require adult supervision," said Deputy Delay. "Dusty is a career criminal and will more than likely stay incarcerated his entire adult life, regardless of this little marijuana incident. Sometimes justice finds its own path, if you know what I mean."

Creigh thought about the justice statement and wondered if Delay was referring to how they treated him with the greed tire; or how he treated him on that dark highway; or how Ray-T, Buckles, and Willy were treated in the jail house; or maybe he was referring to how all of them were treated collectively. Creigh concluded his last thought was probably the most accurate.

"I want to apologize for what I did to you, Creigh."

There was a long pause.

"Here is your license and my phone number."

There was a longer pause.

"If you ever are in trouble or need help, please do not hesitate to call. I mean it."

There was a longer, awkward pause.

"Now get on out of here before someone sees us. As far as I am concerned, this conversation never happened."

Creigh and Danny scurried back to their car without apologizing or shaking hands. The boys were both scared, and relieved. More so, they were miffed at how much Deputy Delay knew about the Hammerhead Gang. The boys had thought that they were invincible but, once again, Delay had proven them wrong.

The next day, Deputy Delay was removed from the Shark List.

12

DECISION TIME

The more research the Hammerhead Gang did on Kent Poole, the more evidence they uncovered. The more evidence they uncovered, the more they realized what a rich, slime-ball Kent Poole really was. He had to be removed from society. They determined that all four of the murdered children were female, around five years old, and had curly blond hair. All indications were that Kent's thirst to kill occurred approximately every three months. The boys knew they had about seven weeks to resolve this issue. Periodically, Nicholas, who had the deepest voice, would call Kent's office pretending to be a potential timber customer. He would ask to schedule a meeting in hopes of keeping tabs on Kent's next out-of-town trip. Kent would often take overnight trips to his farm just west of Meridian, Mississippi. His next scheduled big trip was to Dallas, Texas in September.

One thing that was for sure, nearly everything Kent Poole did was illegal. He was one of the richest men in the south. Along with timber land, he owned a construction company, apartment buildings, and commercial real estate. He was rumored to be the largest on-soil drug dealer in the United States and allegedly used these other businesses to launder money. The research assured the boys that Kent had an enormous amount of cash hidden somewhere, possibly in multiple locations, which were inconspicuous but close to home.

It was also clear that he was unfaithful to his beautiful wife, Kimberly, and that she was unaware of his psychotic sickness. He used his favorite farm as a rendezvous point to meet with adult lady friends. Most of them were from strip clubs in New Orleans. The boys pondered if the Mississippi farm was a graveyard for hookers and strippers. Police records did indicate that an unusual large number of ladies of the night were disappearing from the Big Easy. Kent paid the girls in cash...thousands of dollars in cash. Kent was a sex addict, a deranged pedophile, and a serial killer.

Creigh asked all the boys to meet at the O-T-T. It was a hot muggy night, but he insisted they all show up. Creigh and Danny had done most of the research on Kent Poole and wanted to share their information with the other boys.

Creigh organized everything as if he were turning in a book report. He had it all: names and pictures of the poor innocent little girls; timelines; Kent's hotel receipts and flight information. His high school teachers and college professors would have certainly been proud of his effort.

This was the Hammerheads' own little unofficial trial for Kent Poole. They were impressed with the book report as well and were ready to declare Kent guilty. Kent Poole would get the death sentence and the boys would be crowned as heroes.

Creigh sat quietly watching the others high-five and declare victory for little Emma. Soon, the Hammerhead Gang realized their leader was not participating in the celebration.

Creigh had spent many sleepless nights, agonizing over little Emma's death and what could be done to avenge her. Sure, turning Kent Poole in and providing the authorities with all his research seemed like the logical thing to do, but what if Kent's siblings were equally as shady and came after them? He envisioned the Hammerheads being picked-off one by one by the Poole family. Unexplained car accidents, suicides, drug overdoses—they could all possibly be killed-off merely because of what they know. The Pooles certainly had enough money and connections to pull it off.

There was one more thing, actually a hundred million more things, which made Creigh hesitate on coming forward with the evidence quite so soon. Where was Kent Poole hiding that million dollars? Creigh and Danny could find no substantiation that the money was hidden within United States banks nor in overseas bank accounts. They both agreed that the money was in the form of cash and more than likely hidden on Kent Poole's favorite Meridian farm. The boys referred to it as the Hooker Farm.

Creigh began to tediously explain these scenarios to all of the group. The thought of becoming the hunted "for once" frightened all the boys except John-Boy. He was not afraid to die. His upbringing had been rough, and dying did not seem much worse than living.

The first step of Creigh's plan was to covertly place the evidence package in the hands of law enforcement. Kent Poole was highly capable of paying off law enforcement to liberate himself from trouble. For this reason, Creigh would send the evidence package to ALL the law enforcement agencies associated with the murders. The local law enforcement in Destin, FL; Jackson, MS; and Park City, UT would receive the evidence package. Briancon, France and even the FBI would also receive the evidence package. Surely one of these groups would not be bribed and would find justice for the children. The exchange of the evidence could be done fairly easy and should keep the boys clear of danger. This was only the first part of the plan.

Creigh was looking at a much bigger picture. There was a million dollars out there somewhere and he wanted it. Creigh explained that the boys would split up the money if they found it. This resonated as being very greedy and beyond the normal mode of operation for the Hammerhead Gang. Creigh went on to explain that they would send some of the money to the poor, heart-broken families that lost children at the hands of Kent Poole. This would certainly not bring their children back but could possibly ease the burden of their day-to-day living. Creigh also pointed out that if the Gang had the money, Mr. Poole would not have cash available to pay off the law enforcement agencies. The boys agreed that this sounded a little better but were still not convinced that this was the best thing to do. They were all talking about buying new cars, fishing equipment, and new tennis shoes. They couldn't comprehend the reach of that amount of money. Incidentally, but predictably, John-Boy was much more interested in finding the alleged drugs belonging to one Mr. Kent Poole.

The more they talked about the money, the more they agreed that Creigh's idea was grand. Creigh went into some detail on how they would hide the money and only spend it in small increments. They knew this incremental spending would never last, but they still liked the plan.

Finally, the Hammerheads decided to vote on whether to turn Kent Poole in immediately or go after the money and then turn him in. The vote was four to zero. John-Boy was napping and did not bother to vote.

It was set. The Hammerhead Gang was going after enemy number one on the Shark List...*after* they found his hidden treasure.

13

THE HOOKER FARM

The Hammerhead Gang had a solid case against Kent Poole. The next order of business was to locate the money. Once they located the money, they would simultaneously extract the money while turning in the evidence against Kent Poole. If Mr. Poole caught wind of an investigation, he would more than likely move the money and try to leave the country.

For the past few years, the boys shark hunted almost every weekend. Their girlfriends and families trusted them with this activity and allowed them to camp out often on the beach. The boys would routinely load their cars up with fishing reels, firewood, camping gear, and food for a weekend on the beach.

Unbeknown to their loved ones, on most of the recent shark hunts, the boys would load up their fishing gear but skip the fishing trip and make the three-hour drive to rural Meridian, Mississippi, trying to learn everything possible about Kent Poole and the Hooker Farm. On some occasions, the boys would make the five-hour drive to Jackson, Mississippi to stakeout Kent's permanent residence. They would watch his movements from his house to his office, to strip clubs and to unknown girlfriends' apartments. During the surveillance, they learned that while Kent was a terrible father and a horrible husband, he was very popular with the ladies and figureheads in the community. Kent spent colossal amounts of money. It was fairly routine for him to buy cars, jewelry, clothes, and other expensive items for his girlfriends. He always paid with cash. Who carries enough cash on them to buy a $60,000 car? Criminals do. Kent Poole does.

The Gang had to be extremely careful not to be recognized by Mr. Poole. There were a few occasions where one of the boys was close enough to eavesdrop on Kent's conversations. This was very dangerous, nerve-racking, and exciting. Being recognized would certainly spoil their long-term plans.

According to county records, the Hooker Farm near Meridian was over 100,000 acres of vegetable crop land, harvest pine trees, lakes, and swampy woods. The farm was loaded with wildlife and Mr. Poole frequented this property more so than any of his other timber properties. He allowed clients, potential clients, law enforcement officers, and even a few girlfriends to hunt deer and turkey on the property as well as catch bass, bream, and catfish from the lakes. Unlike his other properties, there were miles and miles of eight-foot fence surrounding the property, but there appeared to be only one gated entrance/exit to the property. It was a very fancy electronic gate with a big overhead light and cameras facing all directions. This amount of entrance security was certainly overkill for farmland.

The county records also indicated that there were drivable dirt roads within the property. Using a plat map, the boys located one of the internal dirt roads that was fairly close to the outer fence and, more importantly, on the most rural side of the property. There were no houses or trailers within five miles of this location. The first couple of visits to the Hooker Farm, they parked their car in the woods, shimmied up and over the fence, and investigated the vast property on foot. In no time, the Gang cut the fence and lopped a trail just big enough for their vehicle to pass through. The fence was re-spliced in a manner that made the opening unnoticeable. The boys could then cover more ground using the car. As a precaution, the Gang would disconnect the headlights, brake lights, and dome light when on the property.

The Hooker Farm had a lodge-style cabin located about a half-mile from the gated entrance. Ironically, the cabin doors remained unlocked and there was no evidence of security cameras in the vicinity of the house. The outside of the cabin was very old and naturally rustic. The inside of the cabin was plush and much nicer than any of their homes. The cabin had four small bedrooms and one large master bedroom. This was obviously Kent Poole's bedroom, as it was the only room that contained personal belongings. There was an abundance of wild game mounts, mainly deer and bass, throughout the house. There were several exotic mounts as well, including lions, tigers, and even a giraffe. Obviously, these exotic animals were not harvested in the beautiful woods of the Magnolia State.

The kitchen and living room were oversized and certainly equipped for large gatherings. There were two ovens, two refrigerators, and a large gas cooktop. The living room had a monstrous stone fireplace at each end and enough comfortable seating for at least thirty people. There was a large barn behind the cabin. Inside the barn was a new tractor, bush hog, front end loader, and other cool farming attachments. Behind the barn, there was a mile-long dirt trail that led to some medium-sized hills, a large lake, and a game skinning rack. Attached to the skinning rack was a large basin sink that was connected to a ground water well. Terrance, the avid hunter of the group, was impressed and in earthly heaven.

The Hammerheads' thorough surveillance revealed that if the big overhead light at the front gate was on, then the house was occupied. The boys figured this was some sort of signal for the frequenting hookers. For the Hammerhead Gang, if the light was off, this was a signal the coast was clear to move about the property. Rarely had they encountered any human activity there. Each trip, the young men would survey a new area, looking for anything out of the ordinary.

One night the boys stumbled across a small (less than a half-acre) overgrown meadow. It was about a mile from the main cabin and located on the property's highest elevation. There was one large oak tree in the middle of this area. The tree stood over sixty feet tall and was easily over 200 years old. The root system of the big oak did not allow much growth, but the boundaries of the little field were clearly defined. There were numerous thorn bushes and briars to be negotiated while exploring this intriguing little area. Large rocks, varying in size, were scattered throughout the field. Closer examination revealed that the stones were very old and weathered; and some had hand-carved inscriptions. Terrance, a straight-A student and a self-proclaimed expert in American history, knew immediately that they were standing in the middle of a cemetery. Terrance explained to the Gang that it was evident by the names and spelling on the tombstones that this was an African American slave burial ground from the early 1800s. Sadly, the education provided to slaves was little to none. The white slave owners discouraged educating the slaves in fear of rebellion. Teaching religion was allowed, and the Black preachers would sneak-in some math and English lessons whenever possible. Most of the words on the tombs were spelled as they were pronounced. For instance, back in the day and in the Deep South, they pronounced "born" as "bawn." As a result, a typical tombstone would read "Tyrone Jackson, Bawn – Novembr 1822,

Dyed – Awgust 1852." Terrance informed the boys that a thirty-year life span for a Black slave was pretty darn high.

The boys also noted some freshly disturbed soil in front of a couple of the old stones.

Terrance, still in control of the conversation, said, "Maybe some animals dug-up the graves looking for food? Maybe someone dug-up the graves looking for family jewels? Maybe someone was freshly buried in the same graves?"

Regardless, it was a sign that someone or something was recently here and that they needed to proceed with caution.

All the Gang except John-Boy were impressed by Terrance's historical knowledge of this eerie gravesite. John-Boy shimmied up the big oak during Terrance's history lesson and was scanning the meadow out of boredom.

"I wonder if there is any marijuana planted out here," John-Boy pondered.

He climbed as far out as possible on one of the enormous branches of the tree, giving him a much better advantage of finding marijuana plants. After not locating any marijuana, he decided to jump down and scare the others. He knew they were already on edge being in a cemetery and this would be a fun prank. He still owed them from accusing him of hurting little Emma. As he was scanning for a safe landing pad, he spotted a much larger tombstone that was significantly different from the others. It had quite a bit of growth around it and was not visible from the ground. John-Boy abandoned his idea to scare the boys and jumped down to investigate. This tombstone was approximately 4' x 7' and had smooth, manufactured edges. All the other tombstones were about one foot by one foot, crude, and had rough, innate edges. Also, unlike the other tombstones, this particular stone was placed horizontal versus vertical.

Uncharacteristically, John-Boy engaged Terrance and the rest of the group.

"Hey, Aristotle, when you are finished lecturing, come over here and look at this stone."

Terrance was annoyed that John-Boy interrupted his epic history sermon but was proud that he was compared to Aristotle. Probably most astonishing was the fact that John-Boy knew Aristotle was once a history teacher! All the boys gathered around the inimitable stone. There was no doubt it was different. Maybe it was for one of the leaders in the slave community? Maybe an entire family was buried here? Terrance quickly dismissed these ideas due to the machined edges on the stone.

To the surprise of the other boys, Creigh brandished a small flashlight from his pocket and began examining the stone. Very seldom, if ever, the boys used flashlights. If any of the Poole clan detected a flashlight, they would for sure know that unwanted guests were trespassing on their property. Most of the time, they investigated by moonlight visibility only. Creigh's flashlight was purposely very dull, and he had to hold it close to the tombstone to gain any real visibility. There were no names nor dates on the face of the tombstone. Creigh got down on all fours to examine the sides of the massive stone. It was there that he found something interesting. The name "Poole" was lightly engraved on the side of the stone. It was very small and nearly unnoticeable.

Was a member of the Poole family buried here? No way. The boys were certain that the Poole family had reserved plots in a fancy Jackson, Mississippi cemetery. Was this a tomb for a wrongful death? The Gang had to investigate deeper.

The unusual tombstone was quickly and, hopefully appropriately, named the Money Tomb. During the next few weeks, the boys made several trips to the Money Tomb. Each time, they would bring new ideas and new tools. And each time they limped away with little to no progress. The stone was enormous. It weighed at least a ton, they guessed. One thing they realized from digging around the edges was that there was no indication of electricity going to the site. There were no overhead wires near the Big Oak Cemetery, and they had not hit any underground wires during their excavation. If a generator were present, they would certainly hear it.

There appeared to be two slight grooves or indentations roughly cut into the side and underside of the tombstone. The boys assumed these markings were from the tombstone mold, if there is such a thing, and continued to dig around the tombstone with no luck. They were all in agreement that the Hooker Farm was where a big stash of money was located. They just had to find it.

14

DANNY'S DEAR FATHER

During this time, tragedy struck Danny's family. His father, the school custodian and friend to every student, was killed in a car accident. The funeral was held on a Thursday and was attended mainly by former students and family. All the Gang were chosen as pallbearers and solemnly fulfilled their duties (even John-Boy). After the funeral, the boys stayed at the gravesite for several hours, telling stories about Danny's father. They laughed, they cried and embraced each other. It was a very heart-felt moment for these young men.

The Hammerhead Gang stayed at the gravesite so long that the "grave-diggers" or in this case, "grave-fillers," were preparing to complete the funeral process. They carefully lowered the casket so as not to disturb Danny's father, then delicately piled the dirt into the open cavity. Once the area was smoothed out, the worker-bees proceeded to place the tombstone at the head of the grave. None of the Hammerheads had attended many funerals, much less stayed at a funeral this long. Nonetheless, they were quite intrigued with what was going on. A forklift was used to carry the tombstone from an old flatbed truck to the gravesite. The tombstone was placed on top of Danny's father's grave and, just like that, it was over.

All the Gang except Danny quietly walked towards their vehicles. The boys thought it was appropriate to let Danny have one last moment alone with his father. The boys were amazed that Danny had handled himself very calmly and well during this entire process. On a normal day, he was very loud and boisterous, but not while grieving his father's passing. They even went as far as to think he must have stolen some of his sister's "calming" pills.

Danny kneeled beside the grave and spoke softly to his father. He loved him the way a son should love a father. His family did not have some of the materialistic things that the other boys had, but his love for his father was real. Very real. This had been a very somber day and Danny was glad that it was almost over. As he slowly gathered himself up, Danny noticed two small, almost unseeable indentions on the side/underside of the freshly laid tombstone. The marks appeared to have been a result of the forklift forks rubbing on his father's tombstone as it was in transit from the old truck. Danny had noticed the forklift waddling like a duck as it carried the tombstone from the road to the gravesite and had subconsciously envisioned the tombstone cracking or falling apart. *That is an expensive piece of rock to be damaged so easily,* he thought.

Suddenly, a light clicked on in Danny's head. Danny jumped up from his kneeling position and sprinted towards his lifelong buddies.

About a half-mile away, the boys were piling into the Land Shark and discussing where to grab a bite to eat. In unison, they saw Danny frantically running toward them. He was yelling and screaming for them to stop. *Ahh,* they all thought, *the real Danny has arrived.* This is how they expected Danny to react to his father's passing.

Before they could start consoling him, he frantically told them about the tombstone indentions, and he was certain that they were from the forklift. It took a moment for this to sink in with the Hammerhead Gang. Once they realized the significance of the indentions, they began planning their next adventure to the Money Tomb in Mississippi. In a fitting way, finding these two small indentions helped Danny heal from his father's death. Possibly finding a million dollars might help as well...

15

RETURN TO THE HOOKER FARM

The ole Land Shark was cram-packed with the Hammerhead Gang and their equipment. It was Friday afternoon, and the boys were allegedly going to the beach for a weekend of shark hunting. As the car approached I-10, there was snickering from the front and back seat. On a normal day, the boys would go south on Highway 87 to Navarre Beach and eventually to their favorite fishing spot—the seven-mile hole. This was not a normal day. The boys would head west on I-10 for about seventy miles, then north another eighty miles on a handful of poorly paved Mississippi highways before taking an overgrown dirt road for another ten miles. They would finally reach their destination: the Hooker Farm and its mysterious graveyard. They rarely stayed more than a few hours. This trip, they planned to stay four nights or until they found the hidden treasure. Hopefully, it would take less time.

It was much more crowded than usual on this trip. The boys had to pack fishing gear and treasure hunting tools. Each boy also had a gym bag with a change of clothes and their own toiletries. Earlier that day,

Creigh dropped-the-bomb on the Gang that he was bringing Willy McClain with them. Although they heard the "IGYB Forever" story and the "jailhouse fight" story about a dozen times, Creigh told it to them again. The boys argued against bringing Willy, contending that John-Boy was enough dead weight for the trip. However, Creigh was adamant about bringing Willy, so they eventually caved.

As Creigh accelerated onto I-10 and neared the Florida Visitor Station, they could see a stout young man standing on the side of the road. Creigh slowly pulled over and waved for Willy to get in the car. Willy lived behind the Florida Visitor Station and used it to take sink-baths and drink fresh water. Danny opened the backseat car door and jumped out.

"Get in. You are in the middle."

Willy glared at him for making him sit in the middle of the back seat between Terrance and Danny. He knew all the boys but was most comfortable around Creigh. Unlike the other boys, Willy did not have a gym bag with a change of clothes and toiletries. Nor did he have any money. Bringing Willy into the group was Creigh's idea, and the other boys were again, silently questioning if this was a good idea. The ride to the Hooker Farm was quiet and uncomfortable. Eventually, and uneventfully, they reached their destination.

The big streetlight was not illuminated so the boys swiftly maneuvered their way through the breached fence and directly to the barn near the house. The Gang went from stable to stable, looking for something... but not sure what!

Creigh had explained the plan to the Gang on their drive to the farm. Creigh knew that Kent Poole's heavy-duty tractor had a means for attachments on the front and rear. It was highly probable he used the tractor to move the Money Tombstone. All they had to do was find the forklift attachments, use Kent Poole's own tractor to move the Money Tombstone and subsequently steal his treasure. Sounded simple except for a few slight problems—they could not find the forklift forks, they did not have keys to the tractor, and they were uncertain if the treasure really was under the tombstone.

As usual, John-Boy was preoccupied and not participating in the search for the forklift forks. Danny had figured out how to jump-start the tractor, so John-Boy drove it down to the lake to skip some rocks. Then he visited the skinning shed, looking for knives and other such equipment; then rummaged through the cabin looking for money, drugs, and food. He found a small bag of pot but did not tell his compadres. He eventually climbed up in his favorite oak tree. He felt comfortable and safe in the Big Oak

The young men searched for hours upon hours with no luck. They had found at least a half dozen other tractor attachments but no forklift forks. It was time to regroup and come up with a Plan B. (And Plan B might be to go home and forget about the stupid treasure). In addition, Creigh was growing frustrated at the lack of help from John-Boy. He was also angry because John-Boy had taken the tractor on a two-mile hiatus to the other side of the property, burning up much of their precious fuel. Creigh was considering cutting John-Boy out of the treasure.

"Where the hell have you been, John-Boy?" said Creigh.

John-Boy knew Creigh was mad because he never cussed. Thinking quickly, John-Boy said, "I went to the other side of the property looking for the forklift." This angered Creigh and the rest of the boys even more.

"We are looking for forklift *forks*, not a fork*lift*, you dumbass," said Creigh.

Immediately all the other boys chimed in on John-Boy's lack of comradery and agreed that he did not deserve a cut in the treasure. For once, John-Boy felt the disappointment of his friends. There was not much that bothered John-Boy, but this was different. Willy grinned at John-Boy as if to say, "I'm glad they are angry at you and not me."

"What does a forklift fork look like?" said John-Boy.

Unenthusiastically and knowing John-Boy knew the answer to his own question, Creigh replied, "It is about 4' long, 6" wide, made of steel and very heavy. There should be two of them and some additional metal bracing."

Collectively, the Gang was tired, thirsty, and hungry. This conversation was going nowhere and was only making the other young men angry.

"Is there any chance that the two long pieces are side-by-side and welded together on one end?" asked John-Boy.

Creigh raised his eyebrows and looked sternly at John-Boy, "Why do you ask?"

This aroused everyone's curiosity.

"I found this big metal object hidden in the bushes near the lake. I was bored at skipping rocks, so I decided to roll the metal thingy down a hill, into the lake. Made a huge splash and sunk like a...well, a big heavy metal object."

All five boys clung to the tractor as Creigh maneuvered it to the 20-foot hill above the lake. It was a bumpy but necessary ride. The young men knew this would probably be their last-ditch effort to find the elusive forklift forks. The boys grabbed a couple of long ropes and tools that might be needed to recover the metal object. Upon arrival, John-Boy showed the Gang where the big metal object had rolled into the water. He remembered the exact location due to the pile of skipping stones at the top of the hill. The boys were all in agreement that John-Boy should be the one to strip-down and enter the alligator-infested waters. But before John-Boy could defend his position of not entering the water, Terrance was already down to his skivvies and waist-deep just off the shoreline of the lake. This was considered fun for Terrance.

Each step seaward, Terrance's body slowly disappeared. It was a solid twelve feet deep just a short distance from the shoreline. The water was muddy and murky, at best. The boys collectively guessed at how far the metal object (it was not even considered a forklift fork at this point) rolled into the lake. As the boys barked out instructions on where they thought the metal object was resting, Terrance would dive to the bottom, feel around frantically for the object, then return to the surface, gasping for air. This process went on for almost an hour. The boys were beginning to wonder if this was just a hoax created by John-Boy. Exhausted, Terrance declared defeat, returned to the shore, and slowly reclothed his tired body. The treasure dream was over. The boys praised Terrance for his efforts while simultaneously glaring at John-Boy for leading them on this wild goose chase.

Unfazed by the glaring of his friends, John-Boy scrambled to the top of the hill and walked along the ridge trying to understand how he miscalculated the location of the metal object. Although the Gang was still present at the lake, he knew he was not welcome on the tractor ride back to the cabin. John-Boy walked alone, and he was ok with this. Unlike most of his time, he was not looking for drugs, money, or food. John-Boy was looking for a clue. He walked about 500 feet and noticed the current hillside looked alarmingly similar to the location of the lost metal object. He moved a little closer to the edge and looked down the hill. He noticed some fresh scuffing marks in the sand. He moved a little closer to the water and there he found a pile of skipping rocks! Apparently for some unknown reason, the Poole family placed several piles of these rocks along the shoreline of the lake. This was the spot! He immediately tore off his clothes and jumped into the water. By now, the other boys could hear the commotion and saw John-Boy diving into the water. Creigh cranked the tractor and headed toward John-Boy with all the Gang in tow. Upon arrival, they could hear him yelling to bring a rope. Nicholas reluctantly crawled down the hill and threw the end of the rope out into the water where John-Boy could grab it. John-Boy immediately disappeared below the water for what seemed like five minutes. Bubbles began to surface, and the boys were genuinely concerned that John-Boy had drowned. How could they explain this? Would they have to recover his body, load him into the vehicle, drive to Florida, and act as if he died on the beach? Should they just leave without him and let the alligators eat him?

Before they could come up with another scenario, John-Boy burst through the surface of the water, gasping for air. Nicholas was still holding on to the other end of the rope and noted how taut it was. Nicholas was really strong but could not budge whatever was on the other end. Creigh signaled for Nicholas to toss him the free end of the rope. He then tied it to the back of the tractor, moved to the driver's seat and placed the tractor in gear. At first, the object would not move, and they figured it was tangled in an old tree root system. Creigh downshifted the tractor and punched the gas pedal to the imaginary floorboard. Suddenly the tractor and rope began to move forward. The tractor had moved about ten feet and the object in the water was still not visible. Suddenly the tractor bogged down in the sandy road and the tires began to spin. Danny and Terrance gathered some large sticks and place them under the tractor tires. Creigh directed Terrance, Nicholas, Danny, and Willy to grab hold of the rope and pull as he simultaneously powered the tractor forward. The tractor tires gained traction on the wooden sticks and subsequently stopped spinning in place. The boys pulled with all their might as the tractor slowly moved forward. Willy was the anchor to the tug-of-war-like activity and had removed his shirt prior to taking his spot on the rope. His biceps and thighs were twice as big as the other guys. His abs formed a perfect six-pack, and he did not have an ounce of body fat. His chiseled body did not go unnoticed. Willy was still confused and skeptical about what they were doing. Regardless, he pulled with all his might. After what seemed like an eternity, the metal object finally breached the water's surface.

It appeared to be the forklift forks.

THE SHARK LIST

16

THE BIG OAK CEMETERY

John-Boy was now the self-appointed hero of the Hammerhead Gang. His bravery to dive into the alligator-infested waters and secure the rope to the forklift forks was second-to-none. This would only be a temporary status. *Surely, he will do something stupid to offset this heroism,* thought Creigh. Terrance was also unimpressed.

One thing for sure, without Willy, the forklift forks would still be at the bottom of the lake. This made it much easier for the boys to accept Willy. Though he was not yet a member of the Hammerhead Gang, he had certainly earned their respect.

Creigh continued going forward on the tractor until the forklift forks were up the hill and onto the narrow roadway. The Gang surrounded the forklift forks and gawked at them as if they were the treasure. Creigh reminded them that this was not the treasure and that there was a lot of work left to do. The boys untied the rope and Creigh circled the tractor around to a position directly behind the forks. Luckily for the Gang, this was an expensive luxury tractor, with an auto-connect device. This tractor had attachments for bushhogging, tilling soil, mowing grass, and lifting tombstones! It was overly easy to attach the forks.

Once this was accomplished, the boys piled on the tractor and headed to the Big Oak Cemetery, and hopefully, the home of the Money Tomb. John-Boy and Danny chose to ride on the newly installed forks. Things were looking up.

As they reached the Big Oak Cemetery, Creigh directed the boys to gently remove a handful of the small tombstones so he would have a straight line to the Money Tomb. There was a noticeably terrified look on all the boys' faces. If they lifted the tombstones, would a ghost arise from the grave? If they lifted the tombstone, would they go to hell? Would they have seven years of bad luck? Creigh jumped down from the tractor and gently moved the historical tombstones himself. He placed them in a manner that would be easy to reset the stones to their precise gravesite once they were finished. He then gathered the boys around the tombstone-less graves and said a thoughtful prayer for the persons in the graves and for their related family members. This made all the boys feel better, including Creigh.

Creigh climbed back on the tractor, fired up the engine and proceeded to the Money Tomb. As he made his approach, he tried to align the forks directly with the indentations on the side of the large concrete mass. He thought this would allow minimal new damage to the stone.

Terrance had determined that the Money Tombstone was twenty-eight cubic feet of concrete (4 feet x 7 feet x 1 foot). According to Terrance, a.k.a. Aristotle, concrete weighed about 150 pounds per cubic foot so this equated to a little over two tons. Terrance was quite proud of his math work.

As Creigh moved closer, his mind was wondering aimlessly. What if the stone broke into a thousand pieces as he lifted it? What if it was an actual grave and they uncovered a corpse? What if a demon was released as he moved the stone? What if the tractor could not lift it? What if it was filled with money? His heart was pounding as he inched closer.

Terrance, Nicholas, Danny, and Willy were standing shoulder-to-shoulder a safe distance from the grave just in case a demon popped out. John-Boy had already climbed up the big oak and, surprisingly, seemed somewhat interested in the unveiling of the Money Tombstone.

Creigh slowly eased the tractor forward while simultaneously lowering the forks until they were seated in the grassy area. As he continued to move forward, the forks slowly disappeared under the massive tombstone and made an awful scraping noise in the process. This made everyone cringe. Could this noise wake up a demon?

Suddenly, the forks would not go any further forward. The vertical beam of the forklift was now touching the side of the tombstone and they could see the tips of the forks sticking out the other side. Creigh took a deep breath, applied the emergency brake, placed the shifter into lift mode, and gingerly pressed the gas pedal. The enormous stone would not budge. More gas was applied, but it still would not move. Creigh finally pressed the pedal to full throttle. The stone slowly moved vertically, though wobbling more than desired. All the boys smiled at each other as the stone continued to ascend.

Without warning, the back tires of the tractor lifted off the ground. At the same time, the massive tombstone descended back to the ground. It landed fairly hard but remained on the forks. There did not appear to be any damage. Creigh motioned for the boys to climb onto the rear of the tractor, making a counterbalance for the huge stone. Once again, Creigh throttled up the tractor and the stone slowly moved upward. After about a foot of tombstone lifting, the back tires started to leave the ground again. This time the wheels teetered up and down. This meant the tombstone was moving up and down as well which made the odds of damaging the tombstone much greater. Creigh was unsure of what to try next. John-Boy, watching the entire process, jumped from his perch in the big oak tree and climbed on to the back of the tractor with the rest of the Gang. This stabilized the tractor just enough to allow Creigh to lift the stone and reverse away from the open tomb about ten feet. Creigh gently lowered the tombstone to the ground and shut the tractor off. All the boys gestured in relief.

John-Boy, who rarely spoke, said, "Damn, I saved y'all's asses twice in one day. Y'all owe me."

Danny and Nicholas nodded their heads in acknowledgment. Creigh and Terrance shook their heads in disbelief. Willy was unsure of what had just happened.

17

ENTERING THE MONEY TOMB

Among other things, the boys were trying to figure out how Kent Poole could move this stone by himself. Maybe there was a counterbalance weight located somewhere on the Hooker Farm? Maybe he somehow attached his truck to the tractor? Maybe he had all the hookers stand on the back of the tractor? Maybe there was no treasure, and the demons were released? Regardless, the tomb was open.

It was unusually dark outside on this night. This made the entire experience much creepier. All the boys cautiously approached the uncovered tomb. The tombstone was much bigger than the opening it was covering. The opening was about 3' x 5'. Creigh nervously flipped on his dull compact light. They could see cinderblock walls on all four sides of the descending tomb. This opening looked more like an old water well than a crypt. On one of the walls, a vertical iron ladder was bolted to the cinderblocks and appeared to extend downward about twenty feet. One thing quickly noticed by all was the lack of a casket.

Obviously, the affixed ladder was there for a reason. The boys looked at each other, hoping someone would volunteer to lead the way down the suspicious vertical tunnel.

"I'll go," said Creigh.

He cautiously placed one foot on the ladder and applied pressure to determine if it was safe. Surprisingly, the ladder was very secure. Creigh placed his flashlight in his mouth so he could use both hands to hold on to the ladder. Creigh now had both feet on the ladder rungs as he slowly descended into the dark hole. All the boys were gathered around the opening. He looked at each of them as if he may never see them again. It was a somber moment.

Soon, they could not see Creigh but could only see his dull light moving in every direction. This was because Creigh was frantically looking from side to side for bodies, demons, or a pile of treasure! Creigh had counted seventeen rungs as he was descending so assumed he was about seventeen feet below ground level. Creigh attempted to take one more step down the ladder only to realize he was out of rungs. His light was so dull, he could not see what was below him. Creigh wrapped one arm around the ladder and used his free hand to grab the flashlight from his mouth. Creigh shined the light directly beneath him and was happy to see a solid floor. He stepped down onto the floor as he waved his flashlight in every direction. He could see a smaller opening, approximately the size of a residental fireplace opening, on the larger wall directly across from the ladder. This opening was more like a horizontal tunnel. He shined the light in the tunnel but could not see the end of it. By now, Creigh realized his idea of bringing a dull flashlight was a bad idea. Creigh could see what he thought was maggots everywhere. He soon realized it was rice and there were insects eating the rice, thus making the rice look as if it was moving. This was a good sign. Creigh knew that rice was used as a desiccant—a means to sustain a state of dryness. He had read where pirates placed desiccants in their treasure chest so it would keep the contents dry, thus prolonging the life of the contents. The rice was definitely here for a reason. More than likely, the rice was here to keep the paper money dry and free from decay. This was an exciting discovery and Creigh could not wait to tell the other Hammerheads.

In the corner of this small tomb was a neatly coiled pile of rope and a very familiar object, a crab basket, very similar to the ones they used on the local piers at home. The old-school crab basket was a round hoop, about the size of a bicycle tire, with loose netting material in the center. This method for crabbing is simple and the Gang had "crabbed" often. Attach a piece of raw chicken to the center of the netting and lower the apparatus into the water. Wait for a crab or multiple crabs to sit in the netting and become preoccupied with the chicken. Quickly pull up the rope until the crab basket and crabs are on the dock. Repeat this procedure until there are enough crabs for a delicious crab leg supper.

However, Kent Poole was not using this crab basket to catch crabs. More than likely, it was used to transport something of value up and down in the Money Tomb.

Creigh had one more job to do before returning to the surface. The horizontal tunnel on the block wall was small and very dark. A large person would be unable to fit in the tunnel. Creigh had a random thought about Terrance's mother, who was very large, trying to crawl through the tunnel. This made him chuckle to himself which got his mind off his current situation.

He could see that the horizontal tunnel was constructed of brick and mortar. It was crude, messy mortar, but sturdy. It reminded him of the old Spanish Trail that weaved through the Panhandle of Florida.

Creigh got down on all fours, placed his flashlight in his mouth and slowly crawled into the tunnel. He now realized Terrance's mom was the lucky one. She could not fit in the tunnel and would not be in the predicament he was in.

Creigh crawled for what he estimated was about thirty feet.

"There is a reason it goes this far. Nobody in their right mind would attempt this journey," Creigh surmised.

Creigh mentally noted the further he went, the deeper the rice. The deeper the rice, the more insects. The more insects, the more creepiness!

Creigh suddenly noticed a familiar object ahead. It was a red wagon, with big tires, just like he had when he was a child. His father proudly pulled him through the neighborhood on his red wagon. This brought back lots of good memories.

A crab basket and a red wagon in the same tomb...Was he dreaming or was this real? Regardless, it got his mind off his current situation of bugs, rice, and very little light.

After Creigh was finished marveling at the wagon, he realized the tunnel had ended. Straight ahead was a solid brick and mortar wall. However, on the left side of the horizontal tunnel, just before the wagon was a 3' x 3' foot stocky steel door. The door was very solid but had some rust around the edges. Creigh noted that the locking mechanism was modern and required a key for entry. Bugs were crawling all over Creigh, but he did not care. He knew the Hammerhead Gang was getting close to the treasure. There would be no other reason for this door to be here. Creigh also realized the red wagon was not there by chance and theorized it was used to transport something from behind the steel door, through the narrow tunnel, to the main tomb. From the main tomb, they would use the crab basket to hoist loot up and down the tomb. Creigh also realized they did not have an alarm system on the property because they were behind fences and the alarms could be inadvertently set off during a storm, as all alarms do from time-to-time. This would draw unwanted attention to the Hooker Farm, maybe resulting in a visit from the police. In addition, they did not keep the tractor ignition key nor the stocky door key on-site. This would make it almost impossible for someone to stumble across the buried treasure—if there was one. All of this individually made little to no sense. However, accumulatively it certainly seemed possible.

Creigh backed out of the tunnel, ascended to the surface where he was greeted by an angry group of friends.

"What the hell were you doing down there!?"

"We've been yelling for you for twenty minutes. We were about to call the police for help!" said Nicholas.

"No matter what, don't ever call the police," snapped Creigh.

Creigh then apologized profusely. He assured them he was safe and that he could not hear them at all. He immediately told them what he had found and what he theorized. It all sounded reasonable but there was one huge problem. They did not have a key to the thick but stocky steel door. Over the past few months, the boys had scoured the farm looking for keys and other such items. There was no way the stocky door key was on the farm.

For two days, Willy had quietly listened to the boys talk about the Hooker Farm. He was still a bit confused about what was happening. Was he really there as one of the Gang or was he there to take the fall if something bad happened? Surely his childhood best buddy would not do that to him. *IGYB Forever,* he thought.

There was a long period of silence. The boys were at a loss as to what was the next step.

Finally, Willy addressed the Gang. "I spent two years in the state penitentiary."

All the boys were not surprised that this had occurred but were wondering about the current relevance.

"What the hell does that have to do with the price of tea in China?" said Nicholas very sarcastically.

Willy shamefully stared at the ground. "My prison sentence was for breaking and entering a house. Fortunately, nobody was home and I didn't hurt anybody. The truth is, I broke into many houses, drug stores, schools, and automobiles. It was my only means to survive...I'm sure I can open that stocky door," said Willy. His voice was shaking, and he was unsure if he had just crossed the imaginary friendship line.

Creigh nodded his head as a subliminal approval. "I have a crowbar, some pliers, screwdrivers, and a roll of steel wire in the trunk. Will that do?"

Creigh was the only one that approved of Willy going into the Money Tomb. *It did not matter because Willy was his chosen one and was going regardless*, thought Creigh.

Willy confidently nodded his head back at Creigh. Within minutes, Creigh and Willy were climbing down the iron ladder. They soon transitioned into the horizontal tunnel. There was little to no space in the small tunnel. Willy went in first and Creigh followed, holding the light. Creigh warned Willy of the creepy bugs, but this did not seem to bother Willy. He had been through much worse in his life. Besides, he was earning his trust back with his old friends. *Not that they deserved it*, he thought.

Armed with the makeshift burglar tools, Willy started the process by first looking for booby traps, alarms, and other such hurdles. Creigh nor any of the other boys thought to look for these items. Creigh was glad Willy was with him. After determining that there were no alarm problems, Willy began to wrestle with the lock. He inserted the end of the wire into the lock, along with the flat head screwdriver. He wiggled the screwdriver and wire for about thirty seconds. He then reversed the position of the wire and screwdriver and methodically wiggled both again. Creigh sat quietly watching his old buddy attack this lock in the same manner he attacked his sports opponents many years ago. After about two minutes of wiggling the tools, the lock turned ever so slightly. Willy nodded his head and gave Creigh a look of confidence. After another thirty seconds of frantic wiggling, the lock turned ninety degrees. The inward swinging door was now unlocked!

Willy asked Creigh to give him the light and demanded that Creigh back out of the tunnel prior to him opening the stocky door. Creigh was confused and somewhat irritated at Willy's demand.

"There could be an explosive device on the inside, and I don't want us both to die if it is detonated," said Willy.

Willy was protecting his friend who had deserted him for over ten years. Creigh put his hand on Willy's shoulder and whispered, "IGYB Forever." He handed Willy the dull light and then shuffled back out of the tunnel. Willy said he would let Creigh know if and when everything was safe and give him the ok to reenter the horizontal tunnel. Creigh felt horrible about deserting his friend and privately vowed to help Willy for the rest of his life. Creigh was really, really glad that Willy was now part of the Hammerhead Gang.

Willy waited until Creigh was out of sight. He then turned the red wagon on its side to form a shield. He positioned his head and body behind the wagon. He then reached over the wagon with his left arm and placed the palm of his hand on the door.

If an explosion occurs, it will blow-off my left arm. I'm right-handed so things won't be too bad, thought Willy.

Willy slowly pushed the door open. For a small door, it was very heavy. Obviously, it was protecting something important. Willy pushed the door about halfway open and stopped. He was listening for a bomb clock, alarm sound, or any other strange clicking noises.

No such noises were heard so he ducked back down and pushed the door a little further open. He raised his head again and shined the dull light into his newly revealed space. He noticed there was enough room for the door to swing open, but the piles of rice (and bugs) were not allowing the door to fully open.

Willy was still behind the red wagon, inspecting the new space when he suddenly felt the presence of something behind him. Willy froze in place. Was it an animal? Was there another passageway, and it was Kent Poole or one of his goons? Willy grasped the crowbar tightly in his hand and was ready to do battle. Picking locks and fighting were the two things he had done most in the past ten years—and he was very good at both. He glanced over his shoulder and could only see the shadow of a person. He quickly pointed the light directly onto the intruder and was about to transition into fight mode when he could see that it was Creigh.

"IGYB Forever my brother," said Creigh.

Willy was outraged at Creigh for not leaving the tunnel. On the flipside, he felt good about his brotherhood with Creigh. Creigh was not going to let Willy die in the tomb alone.

Both young men caught their breath and refocused on the current situation. It was evident that Creigh was not leaving Willy down there alone, so Willy squeezed as far to the right as possible. This allowed Creigh to see over the left side of the red wagon. Creigh held the light while Willy pushed the door until it would not open any further. Willy then vigorously pushed and pulled on the door over and over in an attempt to shove the rice and bugs out of the way. This eventually worked and Willy opened the door as wide as possible. Creigh shined the dull light into the newly revealed space. The rice and bug combination seemed about four inches deep and covered the entire new area. Resting directly in front of them were five large, square-shaped boxes that appeared to be covered in blue shrink-wrap. Creigh estimated the shrink-wrapped boxes were approximately eighteen-inch cubes.

As Creigh pushed the little red wagon past the open door it dawned on him that the horizontal tunnel had been engineered to allow space for storing the red wagon beyond the stocky door. This made Creigh more excited.

Willy really did not understand the significance of the space for the red wagon but continued on his mission with Creigh. Creigh and Willy cautiously crawled into the newly found room and were delighted that the room was much bigger than the other two spaces. This room was about six feet by eighteen feet and the ceiling was about five feet high.

Not so delightful, was the amount of rice and bugs. By now, the bugs were crawling in their ears and embedded in their clothes. There were now multiple types of bugs. Creigh wondered if some of them were poisonous and were they placed there purposely to prevent a heist like this from happening. Creigh focused on the blue shrink-wrapped boxes. Could it be drugs? Explosives? Old books? While Creigh was cautiously examining the shrink-wrapped boxes, Willy drudged around in the bug-infested rice and found a makeshift table in the back corner.

Creigh was using the light which made it difficult for Willy to see what was on the table. Willy cautiously touched the items on the table and soon determined it was pieces of the blue shrink-wrap and a torn-open but heavy cardboard box.

"Bring the light to the table," whispered Willy.

Creigh, busy with his own discovery, reluctantly drudged his way to the table. Immediately Creigh could see that the table was made from some of the same wood planks that the boys had found earlier in the barn. *This certainly connected the tomb to Kent Poole*, Creigh thought.

As Creigh held the light, Willy reached into the open box and pulled out a small package, approximately 1 x 3 x 6 inches. The small packet was completely covered in brown shrink-wrap. Willy leaned over and looked in the torn box and could see that there were many of these brown shrink-wrapped packages. Willy and Creigh took turns guessing at what was in the brown shrink-wrap.

"It could be cigarettes or cigars," said Creigh.

"Maybe it is some type of survival food kit," Willy answered.

"What if it is filled with a poisonous substance?" said Creigh.

The guessing went on for about two minutes. In reality, this was a period of time needed for both young men to build up enough courage to tear open one of the small brown packages.

Finally, Creigh pulled out a pocketknife and opened the blade. Willy grabbed the knife from Creigh and visibly glared at him in this dark little room.

"I'm guessing if I ask you to leave the room in case something bad happens when I open this package, you won't go, correct?" said Willy.

Creigh nodded his head and faintly whispered, "IGYB Forever."

Willy carefully sliced open one end of the brown shrink-wrapped package. He then turned the open-end down and cautiously shook the package. Nothing came out. He looked at Creigh as if he needed approval to shake harder. Creigh nodded his head and Willy tightened his grip. Willy vigorously shook the small brown package. Suddenly the entire contents of the package flopped onto the table. Willy and Creigh stared at the contents in disbelief.

Lying on the table in front of them was a neatly stacked group of hundred-dollar bills. Willy and Creigh could see that the stack was about one inch thick, the bills were very clean, and the stack was all hundreds. This little stack was more money than either boy had ever seen—and this was one little bundle in a brown shrink-wrap package that was part of a big blue shrink-wrap box that was part of multiple other big blue boxes!

Creigh scanned the room and estimated there was over a million dollars. If they gathered all the loot now, he knew the money would soon be missed and they would be tracked down and executed. Kent Poole was a very smart and very dangerous man. The boys had to come up with a plan to retrieve all the dirty money and simultaneously have Kent Poole arrested for murder. Hopefully, this would not allow him to buy his way back to freedom.

As difficult as it was, Creigh made the decision to tidy up their mess, grab one brown shrink-wrap package for each member of the Hammerhead Gang, including Willy, return to the surface and reclose the tomb. Stealing the dirty money and having Kent Poole arrested and sent to prison for life were tasks never approached by the Hammerhead Gang. Willy certainly did not understand the logic but agreed with his lifelong buddy's plan. IGYB Forever.

The Pooles were billionaires and more than likely placed this money in the tomb for emergency purposes only. Creigh figured the landowners did not visit the tomb often, if at all, and would certainly not miss six of the small brown packages. This would give the Hammerhead Gang time to scheme a plan that would give them ALL the money and put Kent Poole in prison for life.

Creigh and Willy stuffed the brown packages in their pants and exited the treasure room. Willy reset the lock on the door. Creigh was super impressed that Willy knew how to relock the stocky door. This was very important because if Kent Poole or any of his cronies realized someone had been in the tomb, they would more than likely move the money. The two best buddies shuffled back through the small cave and up the steel ladder, removing any evidence including footprints, fingerprints, rice indentions, and sweat stains.

As expected, the other boys were angry that they had taken so long, but Creigh sharply and immediately directed the other boys to prepare to place the tombstone back over the opening. The boys were now more confused and extremely angry, but Creigh reassured them that everything was good and that he had a plan.

Creigh really did not have a plan beyond placing the tombstone back on the Money Tomb and vacating the property.

The Gang forklifted the tombstone back into place, returned the tractor and tools to the barn, reset the slave stones, and did their best to brush away any signs that they had been there. Rain was in the forecast for the next two days and this would help cover their tracks as well.

The boys piled in the dusty old car and headed toward Florida. Each of the young men had a bevy of questions to be answered but Creigh and Willy remained silent. Once they reached a public highway and were safely away from the Hooker Farm, Creigh began to chuckle softly. Willy looked at Creigh and chuckled as well. Before the other boys could become angered, Creigh reached in his pants and pulled out the opened brown pouch. He immediately turned it upside down and all the hundred-dollar bills fell into the seat. Like Willy and Creigh, the other boys had never seen this much cash. Creigh and Willy then revealed the other five brown pouches that were stuffed down their pants.

For the next thirty minutes, Creigh, with the occasional help from Willy, explained in detail, everything that happened in the Money Tomb. Creigh gave Willy most of the credit for being able to pick the lock on the stocky door. The other boys high-fived Willy over and over to show their appreciation for his help. This made Creigh very happy. Willy was now a beloved member of the Hammerhead Gang.

Terrance, the self-declared "smart one" of the group, continued to interrupt Creigh and Willy with boring questions about the size of the brown packages and the size of the blue box. Terrance was steadily scribbling numbers on a piece of paper.

Finally, Creigh asked, "What the heck are you doing?"

Terrance snapped back, "I'll let you know shortly. Are these all of the bills that were in this brown packet?"

He asked this as if Creigh or Willy had secretly taken a few of the hundreds for themselves. He was staring at Willy when he asked the question which did not sit well with Creigh nor the other boys. Willy was accustomed to being wrongfully accused and totally ignored Terrance glaring at him.

"Yes, these are all of the bills," replied Creigh sternly.

Terrance was too busy crunching numbers to realize that everyone in the car was angry at him.

Things were possibly going to escalate and not in Terrance's favor when he shouted, "Wow, I got it figured out!!"

"What did you figure out, Aristotle?" said John-Boy. Everyone snickered, including Terrance. He certainly did not mind being compared to Aristotle.

"Hear me out," said Terrance. "A one-inch stack of hundred-dollar bills is 250 bills. I learned this from my Uncle Frankie who has a gambling problem. Each brown packet is 1 x 3 x 6 inches. Therefore, each brown packet has 250 hundred-dollar bills and is worth $25,000."

The boys were shocked to know that they each had $25,000 in their hands. This was incredible!

Terrance continued. "Creigh estimated the blue wrapped box was approximately an eighteen-inch cube. This equates to 324 brown packets. Three hundred twenty-four packets at $25,000 per packet equals $8.1 million."

The boys were stunned. Surely Terrance had crunched the numbers incorrectly. Terrance continued with his presentation.

"There are five...now six members of the Hammerhead Gang." He winked and smiled at Willy as if to say everything is cool. All the boys, including Willy, smiled at Terrance's gesture. "$8.1 million divided by six is $1.35 million each. Let that sink in. We will all soon be rich," said Terrance.

All the boys cheered, hugged, and high-fived. It was a happy moment for all of them!

For the next 120 miles, the boys traded stories of what they were going to do with their money. There were dreams of new boats, cars, and motorcycles. Terrance was planning to buy enough land for hunting and farming. John-Boy, who usually showed no emotion, was excited about his new wealth and asked Terrance if he could grow a small patch of marijuana on his new property. All the boys laughed and did not realize John-Boy was totally serious. Terrance said he would consider it. (Although he knew this marijuana patch was not going to happen on his watch).

"What are you going to do with your money, Willy?" asked Danny.

"I'm gonna use the money to get my brother out of jail. I'm also gonna find my mother and get her off drugs. I want both of them to become better people," said Willy.

Willy's wishes were very different which was sobering to the rest of the group. Everyone else wanted materialistic things and Willy wanted to piece his family back together. This made each boy think about better things they could do with their money.

Creigh sat quietly staring out the window. He had zoned out of the conversation among the other boys. He was deep in thought on how to execute the next mission of the Hammerhead Gang. Barring a few dangerous escapades, the Shark List was fun and games for the boys. Stealing money and having someone put in jail for life, or more likely receiving the death penalty, were far beyond Shark List credentials. Creigh considered removing Kent Poole from the Shark List and acting as if none of this ever happened. But then he thought about poor little

Emma lying lifeless in the Destin resort bathroom. He thought about the other children in Park City, Jackson and Briancon, France. How many more were there? One way or another, Kent Poole had to be stopped. Creigh had to make a decision and make it fast.

18

THE TEAM

The boys crossed the Florida line just before daylight. The sun was peeping over the eastern horizon as they pulled into Nicholas's driveway. They did not bother unloading the vehicle and went straight for a bed, couch, or a recliner. All these young men were sacked-out in a matter of minutes.

Creigh's morning of sleep was very brief as he was awakened by his conscious. He did not tell the other Gang members that he was struggling with the current plan to rob Kent Poole, the murderer, and then turn him in to the authorities. Although it didn't always appear so, Creigh was a spiritual, God-fearing young man. Growing up, his family was in the church every time the doors were open. His father had taught Sunday School to every second grader for the past twenty years. Creigh crawled out of bed and knelt on the floor, praying to God for answers. Creigh stayed on his knees for what seemed like hours. He laughed, he cried, and he spoke to God as if he were physically standing beside Him. He played out many scenarios of how this Shark

List adventure should end. Eventually he crawled back in the bed for a few hours of needed shut-eye.

By noon, all the boys were awake, eating cereal and drinking soda. The topic of discussion was still on how to spend their soon-to-be riches. By now, the boys were planning trips to tropical islands, buying homes on tropical islands, and buying...tropical islands.

Creigh was pacing back-and-forth, and it was evident that he had something to say to the rest of the group.

Finally, Terrance addressed Creigh, "What is wrong with you? Are you trying to back out of this Shark List task?"

Creigh sheepishly looked at the Gang and admitted he had serious reservation about stealing—*period*. Creigh spoke of serious legal ramifications and potential jail/prison time for each of them. They were all still in agreement Kent Poole should experience swift and harsh punishment, whether legally or Hammerhead Gang style. They also agreed that time was of the essence.

Just for kicks, and to try and convince Creigh they were doing the right thing, Terrance called for a mock vote.

"All in favor of punishing Kent Poole for his awful wrong doings, raise your hand!" shouted Terrance.

Creigh thought this was silly but raised his hand along with the other five boys.

"All in favor of returning to the Money Tomb to collect our bounty for turning in a serial killer, raise your hand!" shouted Terrance.

Nicholas, Danny, John-Boy, and Terrance immediately raised their hands. Willy, loyal to his friend, looked at Creigh for guidance.

Creigh clandestinely liked Terrance's choice of words. One by one, Creigh slowly moved around the room glaring into the eyes of each of his friends. His eyes were bloodshot from lack of sleep, and he looked quite scary. Lastly, he was in front of Willy, looking eye to eye. He immediately recalled Willy's plan for his share of the money. Willy needed the "bounty" more than all the boys combined, yet he remained loyal to his friend.

Creigh smiled and winked at Willy and slowly raised his hand. Willy smiled and immediately raised his hand. It was a Shark List "go" for Kent Poole.

Creigh immediately reclaimed the reins from Terrance and addressed the group.

"I've been up most of the night, talking to God, wrestling with strategies, and talking to God some more," said Creigh. "I've come to the realization that we can't successfully complete this mission without some outside help."

This was new territory for the Hammerhead Gang. They had sworn to secrecy many years ago. No one knew of their escapades outside of their circle. The Hammerhead Gang reluctantly allowed Creigh to bring Willy McClain into their "family" but now all agreed it was a good decision. Who was Creigh bringing in now???

"To pull this off, we need to bring two people into the Hammerhead circle. The first person is Karen from Memphis," said Creigh.

The boys moaned and groaned and thought Creigh had gone bonkers. Creigh was losing control of the Hammerhead Gang and had to immediately address his new team member choice.

"Hear me out," pleaded Creigh. "We will all have more cash than we've ever seen. Are you going to hide it under your pillow? Bury it in your backyard? Deposit it in a local bank? The answer is no, no, and hell no. All of those are bad ideas!" exclaimed Creigh.

The boys agreed but were still not sold on bringing Karen into the group. Creigh proceeded with his presentation.

"Karen has been in the banking business for several years. Her dad owns a bank. A really big bank with many locations. Karen casually mentioned to me that they also owned a bank on Saint John Island."

Creigh wasn't sure if the boys knew where Saint John was located. Before he could continue his sell, Terrance, the smart one, proudly piped in.

"Saint John is an island in the Caribbean Sea. Supposedly, it is a beautiful place to vacation and a superb location for wealthy people to launder money. Once your money, excuse me, OUR money, is in the Saint John bank, we can make periodic trips to the island and bring back cash—as long as it is less than $10,000 each time."

The boys were impressed with Terrance's "island knowledge" and seemed a little more intrigued but were still not quite sold on the idea.

"How would we get the money to this Saint John Island place?" asked Nicholas.

Creigh quickly and confidently replied, "Karen's dad has a private jet and Karen has access to it 24/7. She has invited me on several trips. Karen has traveled the world over on this jet, and it would not seem suspicious at all for her to take a trip to Saint John."

The boys now realized this part of the plan was essential for them to succeed and were now sold on Karen joining the group. Creigh went on to tell them all the great things about Karen and how loyal she would be. He had temporarily regained the confidence of the other Hammerheads.

One slight problem was that Karen was unaware of any of this. What if she said no? What if she called the authorities? These thoughts were bothersome to Creigh, but he was confident he could convince her it was the right thing to do.

The boys were now discussing their upcoming "vacation" to Saint John Island. The truth be known, none of the boys knew squat about Saint John. However, they liked the idea of traveling to a vacation resort...with money in hand.

"Who is the other potential new Hammerhead?" asked Danny.

The room grew silent, and all of the boys immediately focused on Creigh.

From a batter's standpoint, Creigh was one for one. Should he quit while he was ahead or go for the homerun?

In a soft, shaky, unconfident voice, Creigh mumbled as if he were hoping they would not hear him, "To complete this mission and collect the bounty, we will need the help of...Deputy Delay. I am suggesting we bring Deputy Delay into our circle..."

Before he could finish his sentence, the entire group, including Willy, were rolling on the floor, groaning, moaning, and sarcastically laughing at Creigh. Of all the people in the world to potentially let in their inner circle, Deputy Delay was the dead last choice for all these guys. How could Creigh, of all people, suggest such a ridiculous idea?

"Hear me out," pleaded Creigh. "Sure, Deputy Delay is a rough ole coot. He treated me very poorly on that infamous night. But did y'all forget about the greed tire night? He had every right to be angry at us!"

"What does that have to do with him becoming one of us?" repeated Danny.

"I'm confident once we show him the evidence against Kent Poole, he will do whatever it takes to have him arrested," said Creigh.

"Again, what does that have to do with him becoming one of us?" questioned Danny.

Creigh sighed. "I did some research on Deputy Delay. He retired three years ago from the Sheriff's Department with honors. Unfortunately, he had to return to work this past year because he was flat broke. He lives with his mother in an old, dilapidated house in East Milton. He provides care for her because he cannot afford to place her in a nursing home. Also, do y'all remember his nephew, Booger Boy Billy?"

The group snickered and nodded their heads.

Creigh continued. "Booger Boy Billy lives with him most of the time because Delay's sister, Booger Boy's mother, is in and out of drug rehab. And one more thing, I was told he spends a lot of time at the casinos in Biloxi. The talk on the street is he owes a lot of money to some very dangerous people."

"Who told you about his casino debt?" questioned Danny.

"I did," answered Willy. All the boys quickly turned their attention to Willy.

"Do tell," said Danny.

"My Auntie is a cocktail waitress at a casino in Biloxi. She knows Deputy Delay from growing up in Milton. She said he has been escorted out of the casino on several occasions because he wrote bad checks. She said just last week they told him he was not allowed back in her casino," said Willy.

Creigh took a deep breath and started his little presentation describing his big plan.

"I will setup a meeting with Deputy Delay and layout all the evidence against Kent Poole. I will show him pictures of little Emma and the other victims. I will tell him about John-Boy seeing Kent Poole holding hands with little Emma in the janitor's closet. I will show him all the evidence that put Kent Poole in the cities at the times of all these murders. Once he is assured Kent Poole is the child rapist, I will tell him about the Hooker Farm. I will tell him about the numerous hookers that disappeared only after visiting the Hooker Farm. Do y'all remember the freshly disturbed soil in front of the old gravestones?"

All the boys nodded their heads.

Creigh continued. "I am certain that these are freshly dug graves for missing hookers. I believe Kent Poole buried the hookers directly over or under the slaves."

There was a long stretch of silence. Trying to get a clear vibe from his friends, Creigh stared into the eyes of each Gang member. Although no words were exchanged, Creigh concluded the boys were cautiously optimistic about his approach to the legal action against Kent Poole.

Finally, Terrance piped in, "OK, that's a good start. Now what is your plan for the money?"

Creigh, trying to make Terrance fill more important, said, "I really liked your choice of words describing the money."

Terrance gave Creigh a puzzled look for two reasons. One, he was unsure of what Creigh was referring to, and two, it was not often that Creigh threw him a compliment.

"Collect the bounty," said Creigh. "You used that term when we were voting to continue or discontinue with this mission. I like it."

Terrance clearly puffed out his chest after hearing this.

Creigh continued after a brief pause. "We must convince Deputy Delay that the money from the Money Tomb is really just a bounty or reward for turning in a serial killer. Similar to the way things were handled in the Wild West."

Creigh's plan finally sunk in. All the boys now conceded to the idea of adding two members, Karen and Deputy Delay, to the Gang but only for this mission.

Terrance, still trying to throw poop on Creigh's plan, said, "By adding Deputy Delay and Karen, we will now only get a million each versus $1.35 million."

The boys moaned a little but realized $1 million was more money than they could ever imagine having.

Creigh had been patiently waiting for this moment. He was saving this little tidbit of information for just the right time...which was now.

"Hey John-Boy, what was your new name for Terrance?"

Before John-Boy could answer, Terrance proudly chimed in, "Aristotle!"

"Well, Aristotle," said Creigh sarcastically, "when you so proudly crunched the numbers from the Money Tomb, you left-out one little teeny-weenie variable."

Terrance looked at Creigh in disgust. He was way better at math than any of these guys.

"What the hell are you talking about?" snapped Terrance.

Creigh quieted the tone of his voice so all the boys would have to listen closely.

"Your numbers are for one blue shrink-wrapped box," said Creigh.

"My numbers are right!" shouted Terrance.

Creigh, still with a soft tone, said, "There are five blue, shrink-wrapped boxes in the Money Tomb. Your figures were for one blue, shrink-wrapped box."

Creigh hesitated for a brief moment to allow this to sink in. He then continued. "Five boxes time $8.1 million per box equals $40.5 million."

Creigh hesitated again. All the boys were staring at him in disbelief. He continued. "$40.5 million divided between eight of us—I'm including Deputy Delay and Karen—will be a little over $5 million each."

The boys were silent. A million each was crazy exciting. Five million each was downright frightening! They looked at Terrance to see if he agreed with Creigh's numbers. Terrance quickly nodded his head in agreement. Five million each was beyond life changing.

Creigh was now in full control and knew the boys would accept any plan he presented. He told them to not worry about Karen and Deputy Delay. He would meet with them and obtain their buy-in. Deep down inside, he was not confident of obtaining their buy-in but what other choice did he have? It was critical that the Hammerhead

Gang returned to the Hooker Farm before Kent Poole or one of his cronies figured out that someone had been on the property. Time was of the essence.

19

THE MEETING WITH KAREN

It was Sunday morning. Creigh jotted down a few notes, called Karen, and told her he had a special surprise for her. He asked her to meet him near Birmingham, which was about halfway between his house and Memphis. Karen had not seen Creigh for a few weeks and was ecstatic about their rendezvous. She immediately packed her designer suitcase and jumped into her fancy little sports car headed south toward Birmingham, Alabama. They would meet at a cozy little bed-n-breakfast off the I-65 highway. The beautiful young couple had met at this establishment once before, but they were with a group of friends.

Simultaneously, Creigh piled into his older model truck and headed north toward Birmingham, Alabama. He did not even pack a bag. As he was driving, Creigh day-dreamed about spending his newfound money on expensive clothes, a new four-wheel-drive truck, and possibly a beach house for him and Karen. Creigh's family was by no means wealthy. He thought about financially helping his other family members but had to do it in a manner that would not reveal his money source. This would be yet another challenge for Creigh and the boys.

About halfway through his road trip to Birmingham, he saw a billboard for a florist located at the next exit. He whipped into the dainty little flower shop and purchased a dozen red roses. The floral arrangement was much bigger than he had anticipated...and so was the price. Creigh carefully loaded the flowers into the passenger side of his truck. He then returned to the driver's side and glanced at himself in the rearview mirror. He gave himself a wink, a smile of satisfaction, and continued on his way.

A few hours later, he pulled into the bed-n-breakfast and paid for a room. All the rooms were motel style with guest room doors on the outside of the building. As he was approaching the door, Karen whipped into the parking lot and parked next to his truck. She immediately jumped out of her car and into his arms. She wrapped her legs around him and almost knocked him to the ground. She gave him several long, affectionate kisses. Creigh melted.

The young couple finally realized other people were watching them, so Creigh opened the motel door and they both entered the room. The room was small, very dated, but clean. Creigh knew if things went as planned, he and Karen would be able to upgrade their choice of hotel rooms in the very near future.

Due to the long, non-stop drive from Memphis, Karen excused herself to the bathroom. Creigh quickly darted out the motel door and manually unlocked the door to his old truck.

"So ready for my new truck," he muttered.

Creigh carefully picked up the beautiful bouquet of red roses and brought them in the room. A few moments later, Karen came out of the bathroom and washed her hands. Creigh was somewhat hidden by the wall separating the bathroom and bedroom area. As Karen entered the bedroom area, there stood Creigh with the bouquet of flowers.

"Here, these are for you," said Creigh.

Karen's face lit up. Her smile was from ear to ear and tears were rolling down her cheeks. Karen was not accustomed to this type of treatment only because Creigh did not normally have the money to make such a purchase.

Karen sniffed the roses several times and uttered, "Mmm. These are so beautiful and smell so good."

Creigh was pleased that Karen was very happy. Karen then carefully placed the roses on the outdated brown motel room dresser and focused her eyes on Creigh. She had a devilish look on her face. Creigh was not sure what was about to happen. Before Creigh could say anything, she jumped into his arms and wrapped her legs around his body just like she did in the parking lot. Only this time, she forced Creigh to fall onto the bed. The kissing became longer and more passionate. They were feeling and touching each other as they had never done before. Karen's skin was smooth and tan. Her body was very toned and shaped like an hourglass due to her training and participation in numerous sprint triathlons. Creigh's body was somewhat chiseled as well. His many years of training for various sports had paid off.

Before long, Karen and Creigh were completely unclothed and making love. Since this was the first time the beautiful couple had been fully intimate, this was a major milestone in their relationship. The intimacy did not last long due to Creigh's inability to control his natural bodily function. Afterward, Creigh and Karen stared into each other's eyes. They laughed at Creigh's lack of control. Creigh was somewhat embarrassed but did not care. The couple smiled big at each other and kissed until they drifted off to sleep.

A few hours later, they woke up and made love again. This time they explored new positions and new techniques. This time, Creigh was able to somewhat control his sexual libido. After a solid twenty plus minutes of sexual gratification, Creigh rolled off Karen and exhaled with extreme satisfaction. Karen was breathing heavy as well. The young couple had taken their relationship to another level. They were still smiling and very happy.

This was not Creigh's main intention for this trip, but it was certainly a bonus. Karen was now officially his girlfriend, and he was over the moon! The couple put on their clothes and were standing side-by-side in front of the motel mirror. Both had worked up a big appetite. Karen would more than likely choose a fancy restaurant that would be very expensive and put Creigh out of his social comfort zone. Finally, Creigh gathered up his courage and suggested they order a pizza.

Karen smiled and stopped brushing her hair. She seductively removed her sundress and crawled back in the bed. Creigh was elated. Although he was currently incapable of round three, he removed his jeans and returned to the bed.

They kissed and caressed for what seemed like hours. Finally, Creigh realized he had not ordered the pizza! They laughed as he ordered the largest, most extravagant pizza. They shared funny and serious stories about each other. They continued hugging, kissing, and caressing.

Thirty minutes later, there was a knock on the door. Creigh opened the door, clothed in only his boxers. It was the pizza delivery boy. He was young, and slightly uncomfortable, standing in front of a mostly unclad man. He then noticed Karen emerging from the bed, wearing only her thong panties. He almost dropped the pizza. Creigh realized what was going on and tried to shield the delivery boy from seeing his girlfriend. Creigh quickly handed him more than enough money to cover the pizza and a tip. He gave the delivery boy a stern look and slammed the door. He chuckled and shook his head while looking at Karen, whom now was brushing her hair in front of the mirror. *She probably did that on purpose*, Creigh thought. *Women...*

Soon, they were chowing down on the monster pizza. This comfort food really hit the spot!

Out of the blue, Creigh asked, "I am curious. Have you ever been approached to launder money through your dad's bank?"

For about thirty seconds, Karen gave Creigh a puzzled look. Her wheels were turning. Was Creigh a criminal and using her for her connection to the bank? Did he recently win the lottery?

"Why do you ask?" said Karen.

Creigh was well prepared for that question.

"What if I told you I know someone that found some buried treasure? We, I mean *they*, are 100 percent sure it was buried by a man that is about to go to prison for life or be executed by lethal injection," said Creigh.

Karen laughed and semi-jokingly said, "So the Hammerhead Gang found some treasure? Are y'all changing your name from the Hammerhead Gang to the Gang of Pirates?"

Creigh grinned and shrugged his shoulders as if to make light of what Karen just said. He decided the best thing to do was stare at Karen and say nothing. Finally, Karen looked at Creigh and said, "You are serious, aren't you?"

Creigh continued to stare at Karen. He nodded his head yes and remained silent.

Knowing the Hammerhead Gang, Karen was certain they had found something. What she did not know was if it was money, gold, and/or some other type of currency. She learned from her father many years ago that in banking, sometimes it is best to know less. However, she knew that all these boys were relatively poor compared to other "pirate" clients. An amount like, say, $10,000 was considered an enormous amount of money in the Hammerhead Gang's eyes. *They probably found a few thousand dollars and are making a much bigger deal out of this than necessary*, she reasoned.

Karen, now in her banker role versus girlfriend role, did not want to incriminate herself, nor her father in any way, shape, or form. She cautiously answered his bizarre question.

"My father owns the largest bank on Saint John Island. If someone was indeed trying to launder money, my guess is they might try to do it in Saint John. Our motto is we do not discriminate on who can, and cannot, open a bank account in Saint John," said Karen.

Creigh continued to stare at her.

Creigh and Karen were having an awkward moment and it had nothing to do with the wonderful love-making session they just experienced.

In an effort to generate conversation, Karen asked, "It is a bank account you need, correct?"

Creigh nodded his head yes.

After a long silence, Creigh said, "Bank account with an *s*."

"Oh. And how many bank accounts do you need?" asked Karen.

"Eight," Creigh said sheepishly.

Karen looked up at the ceiling and was in deep thought. She finally turned to Creigh and said, "OK. You, Terrance, Nicholas, Danny, and John-Boy. Who are the other three?"

Creigh was moderately impressed that Karen figured out the recipients of the first five bank accounts.

He was about to speak when Karen interjected, "And Willy is number six! Now who are the other two?"

Creigh was further impressed. He knew she would not be able to determine the last two bank accounts, so he quickly blurted out, "Deputy Delay is number seven...and you are number eight."

Karen was astonished by the last two names. She knew the entire story about Deputy Delay and well...she was Karen. *Surely this is some kind of prank*, she thought.

Creigh was ready to tell her the entire story. He had rehearsed this story a dozen times or more on his drive to Birmingham. He had to get this right and he might only get one chance.

Before he could say anything, Karen, still in her banker role, spoke sharply and professionally.

"I can open bank accounts for the first seven people. The less I know, the better. Right now, all I know is you want to open seven bank accounts in Saint John. Provide me with full names, birthdates, and social security numbers. Once I have that, consider it done."

Creigh, surprised but satisfied with that response, immediately pulled out a piece of paper with all the information she had just requested. He only lacked the information for Deputy Delay. Hopefully, he would have that by tomorrow.

Creigh wanted to ask Karen a million questions but reasoned with himself. She had agreed to open the accounts—mission accomplished.

"And what about an account for you?" asked Creigh.

Karen grinned. "I already have a Saint John account."

Karen wanted to ask Creigh a million questions but reasoned with herself. He will soon have the bank accounts and she knew nothing about his shenanigans—mission accomplished.

Creigh leaned over and gave Karen a soft affectionate kiss, as if to say *thank you*. Within a minute, their undergarments were shed, and they were deep into round three. The discussions of treasures, foreign bank accounts, and laundering money were temporarily forgotten. This time the love-making session was for thirty plus minutes. Soon after the romp, and wrapped in each other's arms, they both fell asleep.

It was before daylight on Monday morning. Creigh and Karen were awakened by what sounded like some Alabama and Auburn rivalry fans arguing in the parking lot. Creigh and Karen laughed and agreed it was a good thing because they needed to get on the road early. Creigh jumped in the shower and began unwrapping the miniature bar of soap the hotel provided. As he struggled with the soap, he could hear Karen shuffling around in the bathroom. He was concentrating so hard on the dang soap bar that he did not immediately notice Karen's face peaking around the shower curtain. She intentionally cleared her throat, and he immediately lost the attention of the miniature bar of soap.

"May I join you?" asked Karen in a very sexy voice.

Creigh was speechless and just nodded his head up and down repeatedly. Karen pulled back the curtain and entered the small shower space. She was completely naked and more beautiful than Creigh realized. They began to hug, kiss, and caress as the warm water drizzled down their bodies. Creigh had never felt so remarkable. Soon, they were making love in the shower. This was the fourth love-making session in a twelve-hour period—Creigh was surprised and impressed with his sexual prowess. He was more impressed with Karen.

"Are you always this frisky?" asked Creigh.

"Only for you," said Karen.

They both smiled and exited the shower. They assisted each other with drying off. This was arousing as well.

Creigh redressed in his same clothes, which raised a giggle from Karen. She had packed enough clothes for a week-long vacation. This made Creigh giggle.

Soon, they were both headed home in opposite directions. Creigh felt like he had just been through two-a-days football practice from college. Karen felt like she had just trained for a marathon. Although they were not traveling together, they were both smiling big for their entire drive home.

Mission accomplished...and then some.

20

THE MEETING WITH DEPUTY DELAY

Creigh arrived back in Florida at about 10 a.m. on that Monday morning. He was trying to focus on how to approach Deputy Delay but could not get his mind off Karen. He considered taking a nap but knew time was of the essence and it would only make him think more about Karen. He stopped by the famed Milton Bakery and grabbed a dozen chocolate donuts. He chuckled to himself because this reminded him of the prank the boys played on the Santa Rosa Women's Club. Creigh scarfed down three donuts and headed for East Milton. He would save the remaining nine donuts for Deputy Delay and Booger Boy Billy.

Creigh headed east on Highway 90. He crossed the Blackwater River, and it reminded him of the good times the boys had swimming, skiing, and tree rope swinging in the river. There were rumors of all the boys jumping from the bridge together and completely naked. However, there was no evidence to corroborate this event. The boys would also play "Chicken" with oncoming trains. The Gang would stand on the outside edge of the train trussell as a train was approaching. The train operator would frantically blow his horn signaling the boys to get off the tracks. The boys would wait until the train was no more than five feet away from them and then they would quickly dive thirty feet down into the water. All the boys would bail...except John-Boy. John-Boy would stand on the very edge of a trussell crosstie with his arms folded. He would stand there until the train completely passed over the bridge. He was less than two feet from the fast-moving train. If there were any type of apparatus protruding from the train, it would have immediately killed John-Boy. He did not seem to care.

Creigh continued east on Highway 90, past the East Milton Ball Park and the Hide-Away Lounge. Just prior to the notorious Highway 87 turnoff to Navarre Beach, Creigh turned north onto an unnamed dirt road. He crossed the aforementioned railroad tracks and immediately saw a rundown shack on his right. Creigh pulled over and could not believe what he was seeing. The house was missing some of its siding and appeared to be abandoned. The lawn was grossly unkempt, and there were several rusted-out vehicles scattered throughout the yard. The only sign of life was two pit bulls leashed to twenty-foot chains on each side of the front yard and there were burglar bars on all the windows. A police cruiser was parked on the side of the house. It appeared to be the only vehicle that was operational. There was no garage.

Who would live in this hell hole? Who would live this close to an active railroad track? The answer was Deputy Delay and his nephew, Booger Boy Billy. Creigh knew this was Deputy Delay's house. He had done some research on Delay after their infamous "meet and beat" earlier this year. During Deputy Delay's brief time on the Shark List, Creigh determined among other things, where he lived and who was living with him.

Creigh was reevaluating his options when he noticed someone

peeking out the bottom corner of one of the windows. Creigh was not trespassing nor breaking any laws. Before Creigh could decide what to do, the front door to the house opened and Deputy Delay stepped out. He was wearing a wife-beater T-shirt and some very outdated pajama bottoms. He had a scowl on his face and, more importantly, a long gun in his hand. He was bigger that Creigh remembered. He was so big he made the gun look like a toy. Creigh, unsure if this was the right thing to do, let down his window and addressed Deputy Delay.

"Hi. It's me, Creigh," yelled Creigh.

Deputy Delay appeared to be very hung over. He also appeared very unhappy about his uninvited guest.

The stupid greed tire trick, thought Creigh.

Suddenly, Deputy Delay's memory kicked-in and he knew exactly who was parked in his front yard.

"What do you need, punk?" shouted Delay.

For some reason, Creigh thought Deputy Delay would be more hospitable.

"I need to talk to you. It will only take about fifteen minutes," shouted Creigh. "You said to call if I ever needed you!"

Deputy Delay slowly turned his back to Creigh and headed toward the front door of his house. When he reached the door, he turned the door handle and proceeded into the nasty old shack without even looking at Creigh. Creigh immediately thought he failed miserably on his opportunity to bring Deputy Delay into the group.

Suddenly Deputy Delay raised his hand that was holding the gun. What did this mean? Regardless of what Delay's hand gesture signified, Creigh interpreted it as "come on in."

Creigh turned-off his truck, cautiously walked between the pit bulls and entered the house. The house smelled awful and looked worse than it smelled. Delay was already seated at a small, folding table and motioned for Creigh to come sit. Creigh noticed several decks of playing cards on the table and assumed Deputy Delay practiced gambling at home as well. Certainly, he did not host gambling parties in this hell hole. Creigh tossed the box of donuts onto the table and motioned for Deputy Delay to help himself.

"Why are you here?" asked Deputy Delay as he reached into the box and grabbed a chocolate donut.

Like his presentation to Karen, Creigh had practiced his speech for Deputy Delay numerous times. Unlike his presentation to Karen, Creigh knew he must follow through with the address to Deputy Delay.

Deputy Delay was not easy to look at; especially not with chocolate donut frosting dripping from his mouth.

"When would you like to retire; and this time forever?" said Creigh.

Before Deputy Delay could answer, Creigh continued, "How would you like some permanent help with Billy?"

"How would you like a new house?"

"How would you like to put your mother in a fancy assisted living home?"

"How would you like a new offshore fishing boat?"

"How would you like to get some professional help for your sister?"

"How would you like to have all of your casino debt paid off?"

Deputy Delay had heard enough. He leaped from his chair, stood over Creigh and stared at him with those familiar bloodshot eyes. He was not going to take this abuse from a punk kid.

Creigh held his ground and stared back at Deputy Delay.

"How do you know these things about me?" growled Deputy Delay. His teeth were clinched as he talked. Creigh had seen this look once before.

Creigh did not budge. He was not going to be intimidated by Deputy Delay—or at least, he was not going to *appear* intimidated by Deputy Delay.

"Please sit down. I am on your side. I want to work with you to make these changes in your life. And trust me, with your help, I can make all these things happen very quickly," said Creigh.

Creigh's words tweaked Deputy Delay's interest. He slowly sat back down in the flimsy folding chair but continued to stare-down Creigh. Deputy Delay was an expert at reading people, and he was processing every move Creigh made.

Creigh was still uneasy but felt better about the situation. Creigh cleared his throat and began to tell his heavily rehearsed story.

He told Deputy Delay about meeting a wealthy man named Kent in Destin. He told Delay about little Emma being raped and murdered. He told Delay about his buddy seeing Kent dragging little Emma into a janitor's closet. He continued by telling Delay about the research he and his friends did on the locations where Kent had vacationed this past year. In each instance, a young girl had been raped and murdered in that city during the precise time he was there. All the girls were similar in age and appearance. In each case, a piece of clothing was removed and missing from the scene. Kent was apparently keeping a souvenir from each horrific kill.

Deputy Delay, being a cop, was somewhat intrigued by what he heard but immediately downplayed the information as circumstantial and that there was not enough information to prosecute this "Kent" fella.

"He was staying at the same hotel as all five little girls. He always kills right before he checks out," said Creigh.

This really caught Delay's attention. How did these young men uncover this somewhat private information? Regardless, what did this have to do with him getting a new house and all his casino debt paid off?

Before Delay could say anything, Creigh softly said, "We visited Kent's house when he was not home."

Delay let out a long sigh and looked at the ceiling. "*So*, you broke into a man's house!?"

There was a long pause.

"You are the ones that should possibly go to jail!" Delay said sharply.

Deputy Delay appeared to be ready to pin on his sheriff's badge. He was prepared to investigate or arrest Creigh and his little gang. At least that is what he wanted Creigh to believe.

"We found all the little girls clothing pieces, a.k.a. souvenirs. They were in his office desk. He probably rubs and sniffs their clothes every day." Creigh said angrily.

Creigh began to tear up and could not help but think about the poor little girls and their families. This alone is what had driven Creigh this far. Yes, the money would be incredible, but justice for these young girls and their families was equally important to Creigh.

There was another long pause. At this point, Deputy Delay had heard enough to realize Creigh was right on with his investigation. He could see Creigh's tears and truly believed Creigh was sincere. Deputy Delay was ready to call the FBI. Still, the single most important question he had was how was this going to relieve him of all *his* dreadful problems?

"Want something to drink, Creigh?" Deputy Delay said in a cheerful voice.

Creigh declined but Delay brought him an ice-cold glass of water anyway.

By now, Deputy Delay had scarfed down at least four donuts. *Surely, he would save a few for his nephew, Booger Boy Billy,* thought Creigh.

"Is there a reward for catching this monster?" asked Delay.

Creigh paused a moment, took a sip of his water, and said, "Yeah, in a round-about way."

Delay gave Creigh an uneasy look. It was a look as if he had temporarily lost confidence in Creigh. "Do tell," said Deputy Delay.

Creigh took a deep breath, made a hand gesture for Deputy Delay to wipe the chocolate from his face, and began his spiel. Deep down in his conscious, Creigh never thought he would make it this far with Deputy Delay.

Creigh began his speech by repeating the information about each little girl and how Kent was in the same hotel during each rape and subsequent murder. He did this so it would sink in with Deputy Delay that Kent was truly a monster. He told Delay about the Hooker Farm, the missing hookers from New Orleans, finding the innocent children's clothing, and the possibility of many more murder victims buried on this site. He described the Big Oak Cemetery and the freshly disturbed ground on top of some of the old slave graves.

Finally, he told Deputy Delay about the Money Tomb. He did not go into great detail about the location of the tomb nor the amount of money in the tomb. Creigh repeatedly described the money in the tomb as a "reward" for capturing a serial child rapist and murderer. He told Deputy Delay he would have more money than he could ever dream of having.

Deputy Delay listened intently. Although this was not an official government-issued reward, he was ok with referring to the Money Tomb as "reward" money. His current living conditions were beyond awful, and he owed money to several of the big casinos in Biloxi, Mississippi. He, like Karen, was skeptical of how much money was in the tomb. Were the boys exaggerating and it was really only a few thousand dollars?

Either way, Deputy Delay was in.

21

THE PLAN

Prior to departing the "Hell Hole," now Creigh's official name for Delay's house, Creigh jotted down Deputy Delay's personal information. Creigh reiterated that things were moving fast and for him to be prepared to engage in "the plan" at any moment. Creigh told Deputy Delay he would be receiving an anonymous letter in the mail later that day. The untraceable letter would explain in detail, all the recent Kent Poole crimes and murders. It will provide photos, hotel receipts, police reports, and newspaper articles. Creigh suggested he should involve his old buddy in the FBI since these crimes were across state lines and, in some cases, international boundaries. Of course, Delay, a seasoned cop, was already aware that this would be the appropriate route to take. Deputy Delay's confidence level of Poole's wrongdoing was much higher after hearing this information. He still had not been briefed on "the plan" Creigh mentioned, but nonetheless, he nodded his head in concurrence.

Creigh fired up his old truck and backed out of Deputy Delay's yard as fast as possible. He felt dirty, but at the same time felt sorry for Deputy Delay. He chuckled to himself as he thought about how shocked and happy Deputy Delay will be when he "collects" his reward.

Once home, Creigh made a quick call to Karen. He gave her Delay's personal information, told her how beautiful she was, and promised to call her later that evening.

Creigh then called a meeting of all the Hammerheads, excluding Karen and Deputy Delay. Within an hour, all the boys were lounging in Creigh's little, unkempt living room. Typical meetings like this were fun, humorous, and casual. This was different. All the young men knew the serious nature of this gathering. Creigh gave a simplistic outline of what must occur in the next few days, though not necessarily in order:

1. Kent Poole must be arrested and prosecuted for the rape and murder of the young girls.

2. The boys must revisit the Hooker Farm and collect all the "reward money" from the Money Tomb.

3. Then transport the money to Saint John and deposit it evenly among the eight bank accounts.

4. Enjoy life forever.

This sounded fairly easy. But once the Gang started asking specific questions about the plan, things got very complicated.

When should they revisit the Hooker Farm?

The boys agreed that this should happen as soon as possible and preferably just before a heavy rain. The rain would wash away any trace of footprints and tire tracks they may leave behind. Heavy rain was forecasted for the Hooker Farm in three days. A decision was made to revisit the Hooker Farm within the next forty-eight hours. The boys would leave Florida and head for the Hooker Farm at 10 p.m. tonight.

They would arrive at 1 a.m. Tuesday and immediately set the plan in action. The first thing to do is ensure that the Hooker Farm was vacant. Next, assuming they were alone, they would grab the tractor and head for the Big Oak Cemetery. Once the tombstone was removed, Creigh and Willy would once again enter the tomb, pick the lock to the stocky door, and then transport all the money out of the tomb via the red wagon and crab basket. This should take approximately three hours total. If everything goes as planned, the boys would be back in Florida before breakfast time.

How and when would they transport the money to Saint John?

If all goes well, the boys should return to Florida from the Hooker Farm at 7 a.m. on Tuesday. They would quickly shower and head straight to the airport. Simultaneously, Karen would depart the Memphis Airport via her dad's private jet and personal pilot. She would land at the Pensacola International Airport at approximately 10 a.m. The boys, along with Deputy Delay, would board the private jet and the entire Hammerhead Gang would takeoff for Saint John by 11 a.m.

Creigh immediately called Karen. When she picked up the phone, she could hear the boys catcalling her in the background. She thought it was cute and it made her smile. Creigh knew it was a longshot but sheepishly asked if she could pick them up at Pensacola Airport at 11 a.m. on Tuesday morning.

Karen was prepared. She knew this question was coming sooner than later. She had her father's personal pilot on standby.

Karen casually answered, "Yes, honey, I will be there on Tuesday at 11 a.m. sharp. I will do anything for you."

Creigh was shocked and pleased at the same time.

Karen told them to pack lightly, as they would only be in Saint John for three days. All the boys were yelling "thank you" and other kind words into the phone prior to Creigh hanging up. This made

Karen feel even more special.

Who should arrest Kent Poole?

The boys decided the FBI would be the best choice since Kent Poole could easily "buy" the Mississippi state police. Deputy Delay mentioned he had a buddy in the Bureau so this would more than likely be the avenue to take. Incidentally, the boys did not realize Creigh had already handled this problem.

About an hour after Creigh's visit to the Hell Hole, Deputy Delay heard another knock on his door—two visitors in one day. Delay was irate. He rarely had visitors and especially not on a Sunday. As usual, he greeted the guest with his wife-beater T-shirt and shotgun. The young man had a large manilla envelope in his hand. Without speaking, Delay snatched the envelope from him and retreated to his shack. The young man shyly asked if Deputy Delay would sign for the letter. Delay slammed the door in his face. The young delivery boy took that as a no.

Just as Creigh predicted, Deputy Delay did receive a certified letter. Deputy Delay ripped open the envelope. There was a neatly typed anonymous letter addressed to Delay describing all the crimes. Just as Creigh said, there were police reports, hotel receipts, pictures of the "trophies," and much more. This report was very detailed and certainly enough to have Kent Poole arrested.

As Delay rifled through the envelope contents, a small, torn piece of paper fell from the envelope. It was a squiggly handwritten note that read:

> Deputy Delay,
>
> Your share is $5 million. Yes, I said $5 million.
>
> If you are in, call me ASAP.
>
> C.

Deputy Delay read the small note several times. *Certainly, this could not be interpreted as anything other than exactly what is says,* he thought.

Deputy Delay found his police burner phone under a pile of garbage on the living room floor and immediately called Creigh. Deputy Delay used this phone only when he did not want the call to be traceable. When Creigh answered, Delay, without hesitation, screamed at him in a very evil tone. "What kind of joke is this, you punk!?"

Creigh had a flashback of the fateful night Deputy Delay first called him a punk. It certainly did not go well that time...

Creigh calmly said, "This is not a joke..." There was a long pause. "...We need you to escort us to Saint John Island."

Puzzled, Deputy Delay asked, "Why and when?"

Creigh responded, "Why? Because we think you are the best and only person for the job. When? Tomorrow morning at 11 a.m. We will meet at the private jet entry gate at the Pensacola International Airport. We will be in Saint John for only three days."

There was another long pause. Deputy Delay did not have a clue where Saint John was located. His mind was racing with ways he could spend $5 million.

He had plenty of vacation days so taking-off work for this side gig would not be a problem. Booger Boy Billy would be on his own. Deputy Delay would stock the pantry and fridge beforehand. *Billy will be fine,* he thought.

"I'll be there. This better not be some stupid prank or setup. If it is, you won't live to regret it," said Deputy Delay.

Creigh ignored Delay's last comment and chirped, "See ya at 11 a.m. Don't be late."

Delay hung up the phone without responding to Creigh's last comment. These two enjoyed playing cat-n-mouse.

Deputy Delay immediately called his buddy from the FBI. Delay provided him with enough information to let him know this was very serious and had to be addressed by the FBI. The FBI agent had known Deputy Delay for many years and knew this was no joke. They agreed to meet over breakfast later in the week.

How would they deposit the money?

Once they hit the tarmac in Saint John, Karen would arrange for a limo to transport all of them to the bank. Before anything could be finalized, they would have to pay a "fee" to the private pilot, the limo driver, and the banker. Karen explained that tipping is standard for everything in the Islands. She, still assuming the total amount of money obtained from the Money Tomb would be very small, would tip each of the men a mere $20. However, $20 is a large amount of money to island people so this was probably appropriate.

Once the money was deposited safely in the bank, each Hammerhead member would get a credit card and a checkbook associated with their personal account.

At this point, all the Hammerhead Gang would be millionaires... IF everything goes as planned.

Game on...

22

THE FINAL TRIP TO THE HOOKER FARM

At 9:45 p.m. Monday night, Creigh, Nicholas, Danny, Terrance, and Willy have the Land Shark packed with a few tools, a case of bottled water, and several of their favorite snacks. The boys were ready to hit the pavement. One problem—John-Boy is nowhere to be found. The sighs and staring at clocks quickly escalated to a plan to leave without him. Maybe they would just cut him out of the reward money entirely.

Around 10 p.m., an old-style Beetle Bug pulled up behind the Land Shark. The Bug was covered with amateurly painted flowers, peace symbols, and silly slogans. Not surprisingly, two giggling, childish, flower girls and John-Boy piled out of the car. It was obvious they were all high. John-Boy never even looked at the Hammerheads. He wrapped his arms around the blond and gave her a long sloppy kiss. This disgusted the boys. He then grabbed the brunette and gave her the same treatment. Once finished smooching on the girls, he walked over to the Land Shark, opened the door, and crawled in the back seat.

All the other boys were still standing in the yard, looking at him in amazement and disgust.

"Let's go, we're late!" shouted John-Boy out the window.

The other boys, shaking their heads, piled in the car. Nicholas took the wheel. Danny offered John-Boy a piece of gum, but John-Boy declined. Everyone in the car collectively said, "No, Take the gum!" John-Boy's breath smelled like a combination of pizza and two-day old marijuana. Within minutes, John-Boy was asleep, and the rest of the Gang agreed that this was a good thing.

Nicholas drove under the speed limit the entire trip. He came to a complete stop at every stop sign and used his turn signals at every turn. The boys brought fifteen gallons of unleaded gasoline in three five-gallon red jugs. Earlier that evening, the boys secretly siphoned the gasoline from their high school rival's old yellow school bus that was used to transport sports teams and marching bands to away games. The Gang obtained "free" gas fairly often. On more than one occasion, the team bus ran out of gas on the way to a game. How fitting. Afterall, their high school rival was certainly a permanent member on the Shark List.

The Hammerhead Gang did not want any documentation whatsoever of this trip to the Hooker Farm. A driving infraction or a gasoline station stop would certainly be a form of documentation.

Thanks to John-Boy's tardiness and Nicholas's cautious driving, they were slightly behind schedule. At approximately 1:30 a.m., the boys arrived at the Hooker Farm. As the boys were approaching the front gate, they simultaneously noted that the big streetlight was shining brightly. This was an indicator that someone was at the farm. The boys were shocked. They had secretly called Kent Poole's office earlier in the week and he was scheduled to be on an annual golf trip to Dallas, Texas. Maybe his plans had changed? Maybe someone left the light on by accident? Maybe one of his evil cronies was making use of the farm? Regardless, the boys would have to proceed with caution and possibly postpone the entire operation. Postponing would be difficult to do since Karen's role would soon be in motion.

Nicholas continued driving all the way to the spliced fence. Once there, Terrance jumped out of the vehicle and quickly pulled back the fence. Nicholas drove the car onto the property and Terrance jumped back into the car. Rather than parking in their usual spot, Nicholas continued to creep closer to the cabin. It was a very dark night due to the developing rain clouds. All the vehicle lights were quickly diffused.

When they were about 500 yards from the cabin, Nicholas parked the car and shut off the engine. The boys exited the car via the open windows. This was done so they would not make noise by accidently slamming the car doors (and it was kinda cool to exit the car through the windows). The Gang moved closer and could now see the cabin. It sat on about one acre of groomed landscaping. A couple of massive oak trees were growing on each side of the brick sidewalk leading to the front porch. Beyond the landscaped yard was a thick forest of trees, briars, and swamp. The Hammerhead Gang was once again in unchartered territory.

Creigh very quietly whispered to the Gang, "Let's spread out so we will completely surround the house. Stay at least ten feet into the woods and be looking for any clue of human presence. We will sit for twenty minutes then report back to here. Position yourself where you can see the person flanked on your left and your right. Raise one hand above your head if you see something suspicious. Raise both your hands above your head if you see anything suspicious and dangerous. If you see one of us with raised hands, raise your hands so the entire group will get the signal."

The boys quickly but quietly spread out around the farmhouse. This method of communicating sounds complicated, but the boys had successfully used this technique on many occasions.

The house was eerily quiet. There appeared to be a couple of lights on in the house but that was not uncommon, even when the house was vacant. The boys sat patiently. Ten minutes passed and everything remained quiet. Five more minutes passed, and the house still appeared very peaceful. This was a good sign. Creigh was ready to signal for the Gang to regroup and move forward with the mission. The illuminated front gate light must have been left on by a previous visitor.

Suddenly, the peaceful nighttime silence was interrupted by the front door to the farmhouse being slung open and smashing into the interior wall. Two women, one Black and one white, appeared to be unwillingly shoved out onto the front porch. The front door was then slammed shut and the boys could hear the dead bolt engage from inside the house. Both girls appeared to be in their late twenties. They were inappropriately dressed in tight dresses and high heels. It was obvious they were hookers. Terrance was positioned directly in front of the farmhouse and immediately raised one hand. As per protocol, each Hammerhead raised a hand until everyone was aware of the situation. It was very obvious the girls were angry at someone in the house.

They were now pounding their fists on the farmhouse door, repeatedly yelling things like "Give us our damn money!" "You owe us $200!" "We gave you two for the price of one!"

Both girls stopped yelling for a moment, which made the boys believe they had possibly been discovered. Luckily, it was only a pause to light up a couple of cigarettes. Once the hookers lit their cigarettes, they continued with the banging on the door and yelling obscenities.

After approximately fifteen minutes, the ladies of the night temporarily gave up on their battle to convince the patron to pay them. They took a seat on the porch steps and continued smoking while bitching and moaning about their current situation.

Their street names were Lashes and Babbs. It was obvious how Lashes got her street name. Her eye lashes were fake and at least two inches long. It was equally as obvious how Babbs received her nickname. She did not stop babbling (except to light a cigarette) this entire time. Babbs and Lashes were in a bad way. They did not have a ride nor money to fetch a ride back to New Orleans.

One thing Creigh concluded from listening to the belligerent hookers was that only one person was in the house. Could it be Kent Poole? Could it be one of Kent's crooked politician friends? Or maybe it was just one of his evil cronies?

As the hookers continued to gripe about their current situation, they did not realize the front door had quietly been opened and out stepped a man—a mountain of a man. He stood about 6' 6" and weighed well over 250 pounds. He was wearing scuffed old cowboy boots, jeans, and no shirt. He had a black patch over his right eye. He had visibly filthy hair on his face, back, and chest and had a biggie sized beer can in his hand.

His name was Patch, and he was one of Kent Poole's lynch men. He had been in and out of prison his entire adult life. Patch was recently released from prison after being incarcerated for eleven years for murdering a rival gang member. He was tagged with the nickname "Patch" after receiving a brutal shank wound to his right eye and was required to wear a patch over the eye. He didn't wear his eye patch often and the scar made him look even scarier. He had a RAP sheet ten pages long. Patch was a very, very evil person.

Creigh, Terrance, and Willy were on the front side of the house and were the only ones to see Patch. Creigh and Terrance knew exactly who Patch was from the extensive research they did on Kent Poole.

Terrance immediately raised both hands to indicate danger. Again, the signal quickly spread around the perimeter of the house.

By now, Lashes and Babbs realized Patch was standing directly behind them.

Patch gave the girls a smirky grin and said, "All right, all right. I'll make a deal with you. I'll pay you the $200 and let you drive my old truck back to New Orleans—only if you will bring the truck back next week. This will save me from making a trip to New Orleans."

The girls were very happy with this deal and nodded to Patch in agreement. Patch pointed toward the trail leading to the barn and said, "The truck is in barn. It has a few kinks that I will show you but should be fine to get you to New Orleans."

The girls headed across the lawn to the trail leading to the barn. Patch was walking directly behind them. The barn trail was in between Terrance and Willy so they both quietly crouched as low to the ground as possible.

By now, it was almost 3 a.m. and very dark outside. It did not appear that Patch was leaving the Hooker Farm anytime soon. The boys would have to abort the mission and return at a later date.

Lashes and Babbs had just made it onto the trail. They were tired but somewhat pleased that they were being paid and had a ride home to New Orleans.

Quietly, Patch eased a pistol from the back side of his jeans. The ladies could not see that he had a gun because he was directly behind them, and it was very dark.

Patch mumbled under his breath, "Bitches."

He then raised his pistol to the back of Babb's head and pulled the trigger. She instantly stumbled toward the ground as Lashes tried to grab her arm. Patch turned the gun barrel toward Lashes and pulled the trigger again. The bullet hit Lashes in the chest, and she fell directly beside Babbs. Unlike Babbs, Lashes was squirming and trying to hang on to life. Patch stepped up directly over the girls. He was a monster of a man and had a very evil look on his face. He lowered the barrel of his pistol to Lashes' forehead and fired three rounds. He turned to Babbs and fired three rounds into her forehead as well. He attempted to fire a couple more rounds at each girl. "Click, click, click, click." The gun was empty. It did not matter. There was no sign of life in either hooker. They were both very dead.

Almost emotionless as if it were routine, Patch stuffed his empty gun down the backside of his pants and walked with purpose to the barn. The boys could hear him clanking around in the barn but remained silent. Within just a few minutes, he returned to the crime scene—only this time he was driving the tractor. The forklift attachment was secured on the frontside of the tractor and the large loader bucket was secured onto the rear of the tractor. Patch flipped the tractor chair around so it would face the loader bucket. He then eased up to the dead hookers and scooped them into the bucket, as if they were garbage. He raised the bucket to a height that would not allow the girls to fall out during transit. He then reversed the tractor chair, put the tractor in forward gear and proceeded to the Big Oak Cemetery. This all seemed very routine for Patch.

Within minutes, Patch, the tractor, and the two dead hookers disappeared. The Big Oak Cemetery was about a half-mile away. Creigh spread his arms out flat to each side which meant it was safe to move. The boys regathered at the dim road leading to the Big Oak Cemetery. All the boys heard the shots—but Creigh, Terrance, and Willy were the only ones who had witnessed what just happened. They were in a state of shock and could hardly explain the horrific crime that just taken place.

"Everyone, breathe. Take a couple of deep breaths," said Creigh. He did the same. "We must stop this man. We just witnessed two ladies being murdered!" said Creigh.

Terrance and Willy nodded their heads letting Creigh know they saw it as well.

"Where are they now?" questioned Nicholas.

"Patch, one of Kent Poole's lynch men, murdered two hookers right in front of us! He then loaded them on the tractor and headed toward the Big Oak Cemetery," said Terrance.

The boys were not sure what to do. This was the kind of stuff they only saw in the movies.

Finally, Creigh muttered, "This might be a very bad idea. How 'bout we sneak down to the Big Oak Cemetery to see what Patch is doing? We do not have to do anything except observe."

There were mixed feelings about this choice, but no one had a better idea. They all slowly started walking down the road to the Big Oak Cemetery. As they got closer, they could not see anything but could hear the tractor engine. The woods were dense and the only place to clearly see was where the dim road met the edge of the cemetery.

The boys crept up to the graveyard entrance. They could still hear the tractor to the south side of the cemetery but could not see it. Apparently, Patch was being overly cautious and had pulled the fuses for all the tractor lights. The boys stayed huddled together, whispering thoughts and ideas back-and-forth. All but John-Boy. He strayed down the woods line, very close to the tractor. He climbed up a large oak tree that was leaning almost parallel with the ground. John-Boy was about twenty feet above the ground and had a perfect view of the tractor and Patch.

By now, the boys had cautiously moved a little bit closer and could see Patch, the tractor, and John-Boy. As usual, they were irate at John-Boy, but this was not the time to deal with him. The boys were thirty yards from the tractor and John-Boy was less than half that distance. It was obvious that Patch was digging a makeshift grave for the hookers.

Their early assumptions were absolutely correct! Patch was burying fresh bodies on top of old slave gravesites!

Suddenly, and without warning, the boys heard a loud ruckus. A limb had snapped, and John-Boy had fallen from his perch in the nearby tree. He landed in some tall grass on the edge of the cemetery. He was screaming in pain. It was obvious he was badly injured.

Unfortunately, Patch heard the same commotion and immediately shutdown the tractor. He quickly walked over to the woods line, paying no respect to the graves he was trampling over. Patch was angry and confused when he saw John-Boy. John-Boy's eyes were squinched shut with pain. Patch grabbed John-Boy by the neck and lifted him completely off the ground. John-Boy was now eye to eye with Patch. John-Boy looked frightened, which totally was out of character for him.

Patch mumbled a few obscenities under his breath. He questioned John-Boy as to why he was on "his" property. John-Boy did not have time to answer. Patch balled up his massive fist and struck John-Boy twice on his left jaw. John-Boy's head rolled back. He was completely unconscious. Patch let go of his neck and John-Boy fell to the ground like a wet beach towel.

Patch shook his hand in pain as if he might have broken a bone when he landed those mighty punches. This obviously would not have been his first broken bone from a fight, although this was not much of a fight. He looked at John-Boy and then glanced at his freshly dug holes. It appeared as if he were contemplating digging a third hole or could he possibly fit both girls in one hole and this bum in the second hole. He then glanced around the Big Oak Cemetery, wondering why this punk was on the property.

The boys, only a few yards away, where extremely shaken but sat quietly. They were at a loss as to what to do next. Patch was a massive man. One on one, they were no match for Mister Patch. They could collectively handle him, but at what price would they pay? Would one of them be injured or possibly killed? What if he had a knife or a loaded gun? This last question was quickly answered.

Patch, after a few moments of rubbing his broken hand, reached down the back of his pants, and pulled out his pistol. The same pistol he used to kill Lashes and Babbs. Patch knelt down on one knee adjacent to John-Boy's lifeless body. Forgetting the gun was still empty of bullets, he placed the gun barrel directly in the center of John-Boy's head and pulled the trigger. "Click." He pulled the trigger again. "Click." He pulled it a third time and the same thing happened again. "Click." It finally dawned on him that he had spent all his bullets on Babbs and Lashes. He gave a quick stern look at John-Boy as if to say, "Don't move." John-Boy was still unconscious and most likely dead. Patch angrily walked back over to the tractor. He raised the driver's seat and opened a compartment. He pulled out a small cardboard box and tore it open.

Creigh and the other boys immediately realized these were bullets for his pistol. By now, the boys were about five feet apart and unable to speak to one another. They could see Patch trying to load the bullets. He cussed out loud as he dropped several of the bullet cartridges. He was obviously still intoxicated from his night of partying with the hookers.

Creigh and Nicholas were hopelessly flashing hand signals back-and-forth in an attempt to create a game plan. No earthshattering ideas came from their hand gestures. John-Boy was going to die, and they had done nothing to help him!

Patch was still bent down beside the tractor. He was cursing out loud as he was trying to roundup all his bullets that were hidden in the tall grass.

Suddenly, a flash of human movement emerged from the woods and was headed in the direction of Patch and the tractor. Patch looked up just in time to see and feel Willy thrust his entire body onto him.

Willy made a perfect, football-style, form tackle and Patch fell onto his back. Willy was on top of him like white-on-rice...except he was Black. He landed a tremendous fury of punches on Patch. The gun had fallen to the ground and was laying directly beside Patch. Patch saw this and reached for the pistol. As Patch grabbed the pistol, Terrance raced up and stomped on his hand with his steel-toed work boots. Patch let out a loud yell as this was the same hand he injured while punching John-Boy. Terrance then scooped up the pistol and pointed it at Patch. By now, Willy had completely subdued Patch. Nicholas added some insurance by applying his oversized knee to Patch's neck. He wasn't going anywhere.

Creigh climbed onto the tractor and opened the under-seat compartment. He grabbed a long, coiled rope and brought it to Terrance. They quickly hogtied Patch in a manner to make him totally immobile. Patch, half-conscious by now, continuously voiced racial slurs at Willy. This did not seem to bother Willy—he reminded Patch that he, the bad-ass white guy, was the one tied up. This infuriated Patch even more.

Danny ran over to his best buddy, John-Boy, and began shaking him. "Wake up! Wake up!" screamed Danny.

But John-Boy laid lifeless on the ground. Danny slapped John-Boy on the face a couple of times. John-Boy did not respond.

Creigh ran back to the tractor and grabbed Patch's large can of beer. The beer was still very cold. Creigh poured the entire beer onto John-Boy's face and neck.

John-Boy's right eye ever so slightly creased open. By now, his left eye was completely swollen shut.

"Did you really need to waste the entire beer?" muttered John-Boy. Danny and Creigh were so relieved to see that John-Boy was alive.

Among other scrapes and bruises, John-Boy's collarbone appeared to have been broken via the fall from the tree. Danny helped John-Boy to his feet.

John-Boy was alive and Willy had saved the day once again! This incident was terrifying but brought all the boys even closer together.

23

THE FINAL TRIP TO
THE MONEY TOMB

As hard as it was, the Hammerheads had to refocus on the mission. They were running far behind schedule. They just watched the murder of two young women. Now, they had the murderer hogtied, but very much alive and angry.

Luckily, Patch had spared them the task of preparing the tractor for their main mission. The tractor was full of fuel and the forklift was already attached. The Money Tomb was only about seventy-five yards away. The boys, with much hesitation, loaded Patch into the tractor bucket. He was laying in the bucket with the two hookers he had just killed. The boys were not going to let Patch out of their sight. Terrance was driving the tractor, and the other boys were latched onto the tractor wherever possible. Terrance raised the bucket so none of the boys had to look at Patch and the girls. Patch was cursing and yelling at the top of his lungs. Luckily, besides the Hammerhead Gang, no one was within ten miles of the Big Oak Cemetery to hear Patch's rhetoric.

Once they reached the tomb, Terrance methodically guided the forks directly under the tombstone. He lowered the bucket to a distance so the boys could sit on the outside of the bucket as a counterweight and not have to look at Patch, Babbs, and Lashes. Terrance shifted the fork controls to the lift position and applied the gas pedal. Surprisingly, the massive concrete tombstone lifted easily. Terrance then shifted the tractor into reverse and slowly moved the heavy stone away from the tomb. He was curious as to why it was so much easier this time. It finally dawned on him that he had an extra 500 pounds of counterweight (Patch and the girls) in the bucket. Terrance lowered the stone to the ground and shut off the tractor. Patch was still screaming obscenities at the boys. The tomb was now open.

Terrance found an old oily rag in the engine compartment of the tractor. He walked around to the backside where Babbs, Lashes, and Patch were piled in the tractor bucket. He tried to focus on Patch but could not help but see the hookers and wonder about their horrible lives. Terrance draped the nasty rag around Patch's head. Patch attempted to bite Terrance, with no luck. As soon as Patch started screaming again, Terrance synched the rag tight into Patch's open mouth and tied it behind his head. Patch was no longer a noise nuisance.

Creigh immediately summoned Willy.

"Are you ready to do this? Do you have your lock picking tools?" Creigh asked.

Willy smiled and said, "Always."

Creigh descended rung by rung into the Money Tomb. Willy went right behind him. As they disappeared, Creigh yelled for Danny to follow them down, grab the end of the rope attached to the crab basket, and return to the surface.

Creigh and Willy reached the bottom of the tomb, then scurried down the smaller tunnel until they reached the stocky door. Within minutes, Willy had the door open, and the boys were peering into the treasure room. It did not seem as if anything had changed since their last visit—except there appeared to be more bugs and spiders on this occasion. This was probably Creigh and Willy's imagination playing tricks on them.

Meanwhile, Danny found the end of the crab basket rope and returned to the surface. He held the rope tightly and patiently waited for further instructions.

Willy entered the treasure room first.

Before Creigh could follow and provide verbal directions, Willy handed him a big blue box. Creigh pleasantly shrugged his shoulders and placed the blue box on the red wagon. By the time Creigh put it on the wagon, Willy had another blue box. Creigh squeezed the second box onto the red wagon. He grabbed the wagon handle and, in a very unorthodox manner, shuffled through the small tunnel to the main tomb. There, he loaded one blue box into the crab basket and summoned Danny to pull it up. Danny pulled the crab basket to the surface and removed the blue box. He immediately lowered the empty crab basket and Creigh reloaded it with the second blue box. Creigh, in a low tone, let Danny know he was going back into the treasure room to get more blue boxes. Creigh grabbed the red wagon and headed for the small tunnel.

Before he made it into the small tunnel entrance, Willy appeared. He was on all fours and pushing two more of the blue boxes with his head. He looked like a bull, horning a red cape...except it was blue boxes.

Creigh smiled and said, "You are in a hurry, aren't ya?"

Willy smiled back and said, "Damn right. This place gives me the creeps!"

Willy then turned and crawled back down the small tunnel to retrieve the fifth and final blue box. By the time he returned, Danny had already pulled the other boxes up and Creigh had the crab basket ready. Willy placed the final blue box in the basket and Danny pulled it to the surface. Willy went back down the small tunnel and relocked the stocky door. Creigh and Willy returned to the surface. They had allotted one-and-a-half hours to do all this Tomb work. They had accomplished it in about ten minutes. The boys were almost back on track time-wise but still had much to do.

24

NEW RESIDENTS IN THE BIG OAK CEMETERY

All the boys were marveling at the big blue boxes. They were high-fiving and making much more noise than they should have. The boys were especially grateful to Willy. Without him, they would have all more than likely died at the hands of the monster-man, Patch.

Creigh was very happy about the reward money. He would buy a new truck, get a beachfront condo, marry Karen. and live happily ever after. He wondered how the other boys would spend their money and eventually came back to reality. He had a very ill feeling about the immediate next steps.

By now, Patch had chewed away enough of the oily rag in his mouth that he could cuss at the boys. His voice was muffled but they heard and understood everything he said. Patch promised to hunt down and kill every single one of them. The boys knew he would be true to his word.

Creigh finally stepped forward and said, "Here's what is going to happen."

The boys knew Creigh was serious by the tone of his voice.

"Terrance and Danny, y'all trot back to the car. Bring it to the hooker farmhouse. Be very cautious and alert," ordered Creigh.

Both Danny and Terrance nodded their heads in agreement.

Creigh continued, "Nicholas and Willy...assist John-Boy. All three of y'all go to the farmhouse. Put some ice on John-Boy's shoulder and face. Try to find some bandages for his other scrapes and bruises. Look for pain killers as well. Let me stress again, be very cautious and alert."

Nicholas and Willy nodded in agreement.

John-Boy perked up when Creigh mentioned pain killers.

Finally, Willy asked what everyone else was wondering, "What are you going to be doing, Creigh?"

Creigh ignored his question and continued with his instructions.

"Once y'all are all together at the farmhouse, close everything up, turn out the lights, and head this way. Leave no trace behind," said Creigh.

This time, with a little more umph, Willy repeated his question. "I said, what are you going to be doing, Creigh?"

"Don't be concerned with me," Creigh said sharply. He continued, "Once you all arrive back here, immediately take a position on the back of the tractor. I will have the forks positioned under the tombstone. Terrance, I will let you take the wheel at this point."

All five boys stood glaring at Creigh. He had hoped this would have gone smoother.

Creigh took a deep breath. He was visibly shaking. Finally, Creigh said, "Sometimes the less you know the better. If something goes south, there is no need for all of us to take the fall."

There was a brief pause. At this point, the boys could see tears trickling down Creigh's face. "Please do as I say," pleaded Creigh.

Creigh was an emotional person but rarely cried around other people...and certainly not in front of the Hammerhead Gang. However, he had cried in front of them three times in the past week!

The boys now had a better understanding of what Creigh was trying to do. He did not want them to deal with Patch, Babbs, and Lashes. Creigh, and Creigh only, would be responsible for the disposal of Patch and the two hookers. Although they had an idea of what was going to happen, they would never be certain.

"Let's get moving!" shouted Nicholas.

Terrance and Danny swiftly disappeared down the dark trail. John-Boy cradled his injured arm as he hobbled after Nicholas and Willy toward the farmhouse. Willy kept looking over his shoulder at Creigh. Creigh gave him a thumbs up and motioned for him to keep going. Willy desperately wanted to stay and help his lifelong buddy, but knew he was doing the right thing.

Once they were gone, Creigh climbed up into the tractor seat and turned the ignition key. He revved the engine a couple of times before putting the tractor in gear. Once in gear, he spun the tractor around so the bucket was now facing the Money Tomb. He slowly inched forward until the tractor bucket was just over the edge of the open tomb.

Creigh was now shaking uncontrollably. He tried to focus on the horrific things Patch had done. Over the years, how many hookers had Patch murdered? *The world was a much better place without Patch*, he reasoned.

Creigh closed his eyes and out loud, said a brief but meaningful prayer for Lashes and Babbs.

He then pleaded with God for his own forgiveness.

With his eyes remaining closed, he felt around until he found the tractor stick-shift that rotates the bucket. He slowly pushed the stick forward. This made the front lower edge of the tractor bucket slowly rotate downward. The bucket rotated almost ninety degrees. Suddenly the tractor jolted backward as the three bodies fell from the bucket. There was a loud thump and groan as the pile of humanity landed twenty-five feet below onto the concrete floor of the Money Tomb. The sound of flesh and bones slamming against concrete was indescribable. It soon became eerily quiet at the bottom of the Money Tomb.

Creigh, eyes still closed, backed the tractor up about twenty feet and shut off the engine. He jumped off the tractor and stumbled about five steps away. Creigh, hunched over and with his hands on his knees, vomited profusely into the tall grass. He regurgitated until only stomach bile was coming out of his mouth and nose.

Creigh remembered reading from the Bible in the book of Leviticus, "An eye for an eye, a tooth for a tooth." He hoped and prayed that this verse applied to his current situation.

In a matter of minutes, he regained his composure. Creigh climbed back onto the tractor, cranked it up, and put it in gear. He carefully guided the tractor until he was directly in front of the longer edge of the tombstone. He slowly moved forward until the forks disappeared under the massive tombstone. He then shut off the tractor and waited for the other Hammerheads to arrive.

Within five minutes, the ole Land Shark pulled up to the grassy edge of the Big Oak Cemetery. Nicholas shut off the engine and all the boys piled out of the car. They carefully placed the five blue shrink-wrapped boxes into the trunk. Creigh directed them to find a place to hang on to the backside of the tractor and demanded that they not ask any questions. He was obviously disturbed by what he had just done. By now, all the boys could see that the bucket was empty, except for a couple of large blood smears.

Terrance took the helm and methodically guided the tombstone, so it was directly suspended over the tomb. None of the boys, including

Terrance, could see into the bottom of the Money Tomb—not that they wanted a view.

The stone teetered much more than when it was removed from the tomb. This was because Babbs, Lashes, and Patch were no longer in the bucket acting as a counterweight. Terrance slightly tilted the forks forward and lowered them until the far edge of the tombstone rested on the edge of the Money Tomb. He then cautiously reversed out until the tombstone completely rested onto all four edges of the tomb.

The Money Tomb was now sealed. Hopefully, it was sealed forever.

Creigh then asked Terrance to drive them to the top of the hill that overlooks the lake. Terrance did not know why they were going to the top of the hill but did not mind doing this at all. He loved driving the tractor. Once they reached the peak, Creigh asked Terrance to shut off the engine. Creigh quickly directed Nicholas and Willy to help him remove the forks from the tractor.

Once this was done, Creigh visibly sized-up Nicholas and said, "This job is for you. Toss the forks as far into the lake as possible."

All the boys were puzzled. Was Creigh going bonkers...again?

Creigh quickly interjected, "I don't want the Money Tomb to ever be opened again."

Slowly, each one of the Hammerheads understood his desire.

Nicholas was the disc, shotput, and hammer champion in college. He was definitely the right man for the job. Nicholas picked up the forks with both hands. He swayed back-and-forth about four times. He then spun around several times before letting out a loud roar and releasing the forks into the lake. The forks splashed into the lake about fifty feet from the shoreline to never be seen again. Terrance cranked up the tractor and the boys held on as they headed back to the Big Oak Cemetery.

Once they reached the cemetery, Creigh and Nicholas jumped from the tractor, into the Land Shark. The other boys remained "attached" to the tractor. They enjoyed the long, bumpy ride.

Soon, they all rendezvoused at the barn. Terrance drove the tractor to the side of the barn, adjacent to a hose bib. He quickly washed the blood and any other human remnants from the loader bucket. He then pulled the tractor into the barn and shut it off. Creigh asked Terrance if he knew of a good way to disable the tractor. Terrance immediately reversed some wires, removed some mechanical components, and tossed the keys into the nearby thick woods. Creigh was satisfied that this was sufficient.

The boys peeked in the trunk one last time to ensure the five blue boxes were still there. Their treasure was safe, so they closed the trunk and piled into the Land Shark. They soon exited through their personal makeshift barbed wire gate. They reattached the fence and started their journey back to Florida. By now, rain was starting to fall at the Hooker Farm—a downpour that promised to wash away all remaining evidence of their time there. Creigh made everyone in the car take an oath that they would never discuss the night's events with each other, or anyone else. All the boys agreed.

Patch now owned the record of spending the shortest amount of time on the Shark List.

Creigh was in deep thought as they left the scene. He reasoned that $40 million was chump-change for Kent Poole. He was a billionaire. This money was stored in the Money Tomb for emergency purposes. Its absence may go unnoticed for years.

Creigh sighed deeply. Mission accomplished...so far.

25

DEPARTING FOR SAINT JOHN

The boys arrived back in Florida around 8 a.m. Tuesday morning. They took turns taking showers in preparation for their trip to Saint John. John-Boy rested on the couch and chose not to shower for obvious reasons. The boys had outfitted him with a makeshift sling and agreed that they would take him to the doctor once the dust had settled.

Earlier in the week, Creigh bought everyone an old school, oversized gym bag for their trip. He sized the gym bags to contain a couple of pairs of shorts, a couple of T-shirts, some undies, and toiletries. Oh, and $5 million packaged in small, brown shrink-wrapped packages. Each gym bag had their name written on the underside of the bag in permanent ink. This was not very professional but the best he could do on short notice.

It took the boys about thirty minutes to tear open the big blue boxes and divvy-up the brown shrink-wrapped packages. Once this was done, they packed the brown shrink-wrapped packages into their individual gym bags. Willy's bag was prepacked with one clean outfit and toiletries. Creigh thought this was the least he could do for his best buddy. During this process, the boys packed Karen and Deputy Delay's gym bag as well. Nicholas and Terrance were still bitching about Delay getting a cut, but their bitching fell on deaf ears. Creigh knew Delay was essential for their success.

The boys piled into the car and headed for the airport. The Pensacola Airport is very nice, but relatively small, compared to other international airports. Upon arrival, Creigh directed Nicholas to go past the general parking area and directed him to the VIP parking area. The boys were impressed. Little did they know, Karen provided Creigh and Deputy Delay with VIP parking passes.

Once parked, the boys quickly unloaded from the car. Each young man tightly held on to his gym bag. Creigh and Willy grabbed the two extra gym bags that were marked for Deputy Delay and Karen.

The airport tarmac was protected by an eight-foot chain link fence with barbed wire strung around the top of it. Due to VIP privileges provided by Karen, the boys would enter the airfield via an outdoor chain-link gate. This allowed them to bypass the heavy security checkpoint inside the main terminal.

As the boys approached the chain-link gate, they could see a small private jet parked about fifty feet from the gate. Waiving from inside one of the small oval windows was a beautiful young blond girl. It was obviously Karen. The engines were already fired up. The Hammerheads were very excited and assumed this was their aircraft. All the boys were dressed nicely and wearing stylish sunglasses.

At the gate, there was a security guard standing behind a makeshift wooden podium. He was young and had a clipboard in his hand. He appeared a bit awkward as if he was a relatively new employee. It made further sense that the low-man on the totem pole would have to stand outside in the hot sun all day.

A few steps away stood a very large man with a very large pot belly. He was wearing a pair of white trousers, a white vest, and a blue button-down silk shirt. He had a cowboy-style hat on his head, cowboy boots, gold-rimmed sunglasses, and a toothpick in his mouth. It was none other than Deputy Delay.

Creigh immediately walked up to Deputy Delay, dropped his gym bag, and extended his hand. Delay, maintaining a stern look on his face, shook his hand without speaking. Deputy Delay glanced at the other boys and nodded his head as if to say, "Hello, but I'm not shaking your hands."

Deputy Delay was looking sharp. All the boys admired his new look. They were all still very cautious and scared of him.

"Let's get going," said Creigh. Creigh handed Delay the extra gym bag and stepped up to the security station.

The young security officer smiled and said "Hello" to Creigh. Creigh smiled back.

"What is your destination, sir?" asked the security guard.

"Saint John Island," answered Creigh.

"Are all of you traveling together?" asked the guard.

"Yes," replied Creigh.

The security guard had a list with all their names on it.

"I need to see your IDs," said the security guard.

All the boys pulled out their wallets and handed the security guard their driver's licenses. For a brief moment, Creigh had a sinking feeling. *Does Willy have a license?*

Surprisingly, Willy pulled out a license and handed it to the security guard. Willy could sense Creigh looking at him.

"Are you really that surprised?" asked Willy. Creigh turned his head and tried to downplay his reaction of disbelief.

"Some of us have licenses," snapped Willy. He shook his head in disgust at Creigh.

"I love you man," said Creigh.

Willy smiled and said, "IGYB Forever."

Creigh smiled and was relieved that all was well between them.

The security guard checked each license against the names Karen provided on the list. All the information was accurate, and the security guard returned the driver's licenses.

Creigh repocketed his license and picked up his gym bag. He took two steps toward the aircraft. The rest of the Gang was following his lead.

Unexpectedly, the security officer raised his voice and yelled, "STOP!"

Creigh immediately stopped in his tracks.

"Is there a problem?" Creigh asked.

"I need to check your bags," snipped the young security guard.

Creigh stared at the guard in disbelief. Karen had been adamant about there not being a baggage check at the private jet gate. He knew this young guy was stepping beyond the scope of his work statement. He also knew if he demanded Creigh open one of the brown shrink-wrapped packages all their plans would be foiled. Somehow, they might trace the money back to Kent Poole and he would be charged with the murder of Patch. Creigh felt sick to his stomach.

Suddenly, the security guard disappeared from Creigh's view. It was not because he had moved. It was because Deputy Delay had stepped between them. Deputy Delay pulled off his sunglasses and lowered his head to the level of the young security guard. He stared at him with those same bloodshot eyes Creigh had seen on too many occasions. With his other hand, he reached in his vest pocket and pulled out a very shiny badge. Deputy Delay held the badge about six inches from the young man's face. Delay's scowling face was about three inches behind the badge, which was even scarier.

"Do you know what this says?" snapped Deputy Delay.

By now, the young security guard was visibly shaking.

"Police?" answered the young man.

Deputy Delay moved a little closer to the young man.

"It says Federal Bureau of Investigation. Do you know what that means, punk?" barked Deputy Delay.

Creigh quietly snickered when he heard the word "punk."

"Yes sir, I do," said the young security guard.

Deputy Delay looked from side to side and then his voice got eerily quieter.

"This trip is official government business. Which would you rather do? Number one, get fired from your job and have your record tarnished forever for tampering with a government operation? Or number two, let us on our plane as per protocol."

The young man knew nothing about government protocol but immediately said, "Number two."

Deputy Delay put his badge back into his vest pocket. Obviously, he had "borrowed" the badge from his FBI buddy. He continued to stare at the young security guard.

The Hammerheads gathered up their gym bags and headed for the plane. The aircraft door was open, and the boarding ladder was extended from the aircraft.

One by one, they made their way into the private jet. It was a slow process because Karen was seated next to the door and each Hammerhead had to greet her with a big hug. She was shocked to see the damage to John-Boy's face and immediately tried to comfort him. He insisted he was fine and continued to the back of the aircraft.

"This is freakin' sweet," Danny whistled, tossing his duffel bag onto an open seat.

"Dang this is livin'," he added snuggling into the oversized leather seat.

Luckily, Karen had prepared and bought the boys some clothes. Each member dressed in pleated shorts, new sandals, and some Hawaiian patterned shirt for the trip to the islands. "You all need to look the part," Karen instructed. "No one's going to believe you if you show up looking like a bunch of homeless people," she jeered. Everyone seemed to appreciate the new style, except for John-Boy, who cringed as he pulled over the pink, Hawaiian shirt.

The airfield was very loud due to the dual engines on their private jet and the proximity to the commercial jets taxiing on the nearby runway. Deputy Delay and Creigh were still standing on the tarmac. There was a big gap between Deputy Delay and the Hammerheads that boarded the aircraft in front of him. Creigh felt weird and knew something was not right. Finally, Deputy Delay turned around, put his large hand on Creigh's shoulder, and shouted over the roaring engine, "I am not going to Saint John!"

There was a long pause. Creigh was certainly confused.

"Why not!?" asked Creigh.

Deputy Delay looked at Creigh with a sad face. Creigh had never seen this expression before.

"This is goodbye forever . . . As far as the world knows, you and I have never crossed paths!" said Deputy Delay.

Again, Creigh asked, "Why!?"

Deputy Delay moved closer to Creigh to ensure Creigh heard and understood everything he said.

"Once all this breaks, the FBI will work tirelessly to determine who sent me the anonymous letter. Currently, there is nothing that ties you and your buddies to me. I will doctor-up the anonymous letter to send the FBI in another direction. Billy and I will move north. Maybe

Canada or one of the bordering states. I will pay off my debts and be able to get solid, professional help for Billy," said Delay.

By now, Creigh understood why this had to happen but was still very sad.

Once again, tears were rolling down Creigh's face. Creigh stuck out his hand for a farewell handshake. Instead, Deputy Delay wrapped his arms around Creigh and gave him a monstrous bear hug. It lasted about thirty seconds. Finally Delay released him and took a step backward. Creigh could now see the tears rolling down Delay's wrinkled cheeks.

"You are crying," said Creigh.

"No, I'm not!" snapped Deputy Delay.

"I'll never forget you," said Creigh.

"Get your scrawny ass on the plane!" said Delay.

Creigh smiled and scurried up the boarding ladder. He immediately saw Karen and gave her a big hug and a juicy kiss. Creigh could see out the window over Karen's shoulder. Deputy Delay, with gym bag in hand and cowboy hat on his head, was walking past the young security guard and to the parking lot.

"Where is he going?" asked Terrance.

"Who?" said Creigh.

Terrance pointed out the window at Deputy Delay.

"I do not know that man. None of us know that man. We have never crossed paths with that man," said Creigh in a loud voice for everyone to hear.

Confused, Terrance said, "But I don't understand."

The other boys seemed a bit baffled as well.

Creigh, addressing the entire group, said very sharply. "Again, I do not know that man. None of us know that man. We have never crossed paths with that man. Furthermore, we will never *ever* try to contact that man nor speak of that man. Do you remember taking an oath? Am I clear?"

All the boys now seemed to understand what Creigh was saying and nodded their heads.

Before Karen could shut the boarding door, John-Boy, who was unable to stand on his own, raised his hand and said, "If Delay does not have to go, then I don't want to go! I have heard bad things about that place and would rather take my share of the money and go home!"

Willy chimed in as well. "I'm scared to fly and have no interest in Saint John. I want to stay here. This is my home. If Delay can stay, why can't I stay?"

Creigh quickly jumped from his seat. He stood in between John-Boy and Willy, glaring at both boys.

"Listen here! You are both going to Saint John. End of story! If you don't want to go, then get off this plane right now—but you will not receive one dime of the reward money. Zero! Zilch! We all agreed to this plan!"

There was a short pause.

"Furthermore, I just told the entire group to never mention that man ever again and you both said his name within two minutes!"

There was another short pause.

Finally, in a softer tone, Creigh continued, "Sit back and enjoy the flight. We will only be there a couple of days. We've made it this far. Don't screw this up for all of us."

The other boys agreed with Creigh and reassured John-Boy and Willy that everything would go smoothly.

"Fine, I'll go. But I want to come home as soon as possible," snipped John-Boy.

Willy nodded in agreement with John-Boy.

"Good," said Creigh. "Once we take care of business, I'll see about getting you guys a flight home sooner than the rest of us."

Willy and John-Boy reluctantly nodded in agreement.

Immediately following this impromptu discussion, Karen closed and latched the boarding door. She wasn't sure what Creigh meant in his brief little speech, but she certainly expected an explanation later.

"There are drinks, right?" asked Terrence.

"Yes, there are. I'll get everyone a shot," answered Karen. Everyone was settled in their seat and Karen appeared with a tray of shots.

"To new beginnings," she announced, raising the glass of vodka. Everyone agreed and shot back the burning alcohol.

"We are ready to go," the pilot announced to Karen. She nodded, taking her seat next to Creigh and buckling the latch across her waist. All the Hammerheads fastened their seatbelts and prepared for takeoff. Across from him, Creigh noticed Willy gripping the seat handles. It was obvious he had never flown before. He was visibly shaking, and his eyes were tightly squeezed shut.

Creigh reached over and put his hand on Willy's shoulder and said, "IGYB Forever."

Willy looked up and said, "That sounds nice and all but you ain't the one flying this damn plane."

All the boys laughed at Willy's comment, and this seemed to comfort Willy. He smiled but immediately returned to his squinty-eye posture.

The jet vibrated beneath them, the dual engines humming loudly outside the windows as the private jet slowly taxied to one end of the runway.

The pilot turned the aircraft 180 degrees and was now facing the long stretch of asphalt. Within seconds, the aircraft was speeding down the runway. The truth be known, none of the boys were experienced fliers and they all maintained a posture similar to Willy. Soon, wheels were up, and the aircraft was ascending in the air. Occasionally, the small jet would rock or shutter due to the turbulence from the breezy day. All the boys looked to Karen for assurance that everything was fine.

Once they reached a desired altitude, the pilot leveled-off the aircraft. The remainder of the flight to Saint John was calm and flawless. Karen snuggled up to Creigh, but he was deep in thought...Now, Creigh knew Karen had money, but he never wanted her to think it was important to him. He was with Karen because he loved her, end of story. For the rest of the flight all the boys catnapped. Their long night at the Hooker Farm had finally caught up with them.

A few hours later, the pilot announced their descent into Saint John. The downward turn and subsequent landing of the aircraft was much bumpier than all the Gang anticipated. This turbulence made everyone look Karen's way for reassurance. Once the aircraft came to a stop, Karen mechanically unlatched the door and extended the steps. It was obvious she had done this on many occasions. Karen stood at the door as the boys gathered up their belongings, which consisted of identical gym bags, and headed down the steps. Luckily, Willy was there to help John-Boy down the steps.

Other than the pilot, Creigh and Karen were the last people still on the private jet. Rather than proceed down the steps as the others did, Creigh by-passed the door and popped his head into the cockpit.

"Thank you for getting us here safely," said Creigh.

The pilot was still doing pilot things but took the time to smile and acknowledge Creigh's kind words. Creigh then handed the pilot a fist full of hundred-dollar bills. The pilot was pleasantly surprised. Normally, he received a twenty to fifty dollar tip, if anything, for each of his trips. This appeared to be, at the least, a thousand. He smiled even bigger and thanked Creigh several more times.

Karen saw this entire interaction take place between Creigh and the pilot. She was still unaware of how much money the boys had in their gym bags. However, at this point, she realized it was more than a few thousand dollars.

She glared at Creigh and said, "We need to talk."

He smiled and nodded his head as they departed the plane.

26

BANKING IN
SAINT JOHN

Still in the airport, Karen immediately summoned a local security company in Saint John that her father used often. The security company was located close to the airport, and it was obvious the Gang needed extra security, even if it was only a short trip from the airport to the bank. Each boy had one piece of luggage—a gym bag. Unlike the boys, Karen had four suitcases of various sizes, a make-up bag, a beach bag, and a purse big enough to carry a bushel of pineapples. Seven bags for three days! Seven bags!! The boys laughed and made jokes about her excessive luggage but gladly helped her carry them.

Surprisingly, Karen and the guys made it smoothly through the airport. This was more than likely due to the generous tips the boys provided along the way.

Karen's plan was to catch a puddle jumper over to Cruz Bay and then a limo to the Trustworthy Saint John Bank. However, the resistance from John-Boy and Willy was too great to even attempt to board another plane. She knew this might happen and had made backup plans with a ferry service. The ferry was a bit more than walking distance from the airport, but the boys did not mind. The fresh air was nice, and the scenery was incredible. The gym bags were clutched tightly in the hands of each Hammerhead. Also, each young man was carrying one of Karen's multiple bags. They looked like a band of American Gypsies walking to the ferryboat.

Soon, the Gang reached their next destination. With luggage and gym bags in hand, the Hammerheads trotted across the catwalk as the sound of the ferry whistle echoed through the air. Within minutes, the ferry was untethered from the wharf and making its way to Cruz Bay. Creigh marveled at the crystal blue waters and the perfect weather. The fresh air was nice, and the scenery was incredible. There were free snacks and drinks available to the passengers. The young men certainly took advantage of this pleasantry.

Karen led the Gang to the top level of the ferry, which was devoid of anyone mostly due to the fierce winds at this height. Creigh liked her choice of space, wanting to keep a low profile and avoid other people. He was slightly nervous with millions of dollars in their gym bags.

Most of the Gang rushed to the railings, tossing their hands up and pretending as if they were flying. Creigh even heard Danny yell, "I'm king of the world!" Of course, none of them would admit to knowing a line from the *Titanic*, but they did all chuckle at the secret. Karen and Creigh snuggled together on the opposite end, gazing out over the smooth clear waters. Then Creigh noticed Willy sitting in the dead center of the deck.

Willy was clearly uneasy about being on a boat and Creigh remembered him saying he couldn't swim. Pushing away from Karen, Creigh made his way over to his friend. "You okay?"

"Fine," he lied.

"Here." Karen emerged, sitting next to him, and reaching under the seat to pull out a lifejacket. Willy's eyes widened. Creigh knew there was no way he'd wear that thing in front of everyone.

Karen pulled the lifejacket over her shoulders. "I am a terrible swimmer and just don't want to take any chances," she explained to Willy. She reached under the seat and pulled out another life jacket. "Don't make me look silly," she said, motioning for Willy to put it on.

"Yeah, sure thing."

The truth of the matter was Karen was a terrific swimmer. In fact, she swam competitively on her college swim team for four years. She only did this kind gesture to put Willy at ease. Creigh reached under the seat next to Karen and pulled a lifejacket over his own shoulders.

"IGYB Forever buddy," added Creigh.

The water was slick as glass making for a smooth ride over to Saint John Island. After a brief time on the top deck, most of the Gang descended to the cabin to take advantage of the free food Karen had mentioned. The Gang ate and drank all of the snacks on the boat. Every single crumb. This was uncommon and annoyed the captain and his mate. Regardless, they smiled and showed no signs of disgust.

The ferryboat eventually pulled up alongside an old wooden dock. The crew member secured the dock line to the ferryboat and opened the ferry door.

As the boys debarked from the ferryboat, each one gave a very generous tip to the captain and his mate. It was more than generous. It was the biggest tip they ever received. This certainly made up for the earlier snack-fest.

Willy continued to wear his life vest until he was safely on solid land. Likewise, Creigh and Karen did the same thing. The threesome removed the lifejackets and Creigh returned them to the boat. By now, the captain and his mate had counted their tip money. They smiled big at Creigh and hugged his neck. All the Gang could see this interaction and it made them very happy. They made the captain and his mate feel appreciated and, at the same time, the captain and his mate made them feel appreciated. It was a win for everybody.

As they exited the small, quaint marina, they could see a pair of black stretch SUVs parked on the curb. Karen directed the boys to divide up and grab a seat in the vehicles. The driver of each vehicle tried to accommodate the boys by offering to place their gym bags into the luggage section of the SUV. All the boys declined and maintained a tight grip on their gym bags. The drivers distributed Karen's luggage between both vehicles. This was probably done so both drivers would receive a tip.

All the Hammerheads piled into the stretch SUVs. The drivers were prepared to make the short drive to the bank. Suddenly, a third SUV zoomed up and blocked them into the curb. All the boys were on high alert and were not sure what was about to happen.

Two Island men emerged from the back seat of the third SUV. They were very fit, nice looking, and appeared to be a few years older than the boys. They were dressed alike in tight aqua blue collared shirts, short white pants, and clean white tennis shoes.

Before anyone could say a word, the men piled into the front seat of each SUV and the third SUV swiftly departed. The boys were unsure if this was a heist and clutched their gym bags even tighter.

After a very brief moment, Karen, who was in the front stretch SUV, asked their newest passenger for some identification. In an effort to not startle anyone, he raised one hand in the air and slowly pulled his wallet from his pants pocket with his other hand. He then flipped the wallet open, and everyone could see a shiny badge. He then pulled a business card from the wallet and handed it to Karen. As Karen expected, he was from the security company. He carried a badge because he worked fulltime for the police department. Moonlighting as a bodyguard was a parttime gig but paid very well.

Karen turned to the stretch SUV behind her and gave them a thumbs up. The boys were not keen with the new bodyguards and thought it was overkill. Or even worse, they could be crooks. Nonetheless, the security guards were in the SUVs and now part of the team.

Karen then directed the driver to take them to the Trustworthy Saint John Bank. Karen and her father held accounts at this bank for many years. Her father was on the Board of Trustees and was well-respected at the Trustworthy Saint John Bank.

Sitting next to Karen in the back of the SUV, Creigh slid his fingers between her own, taking note of the bright red color on her nails. For a moment, he envisioned a massive diamond ring on her finger as his thumb and index finger gently rubbed her own. Looking up at him, it was as if she had read his mind, a sly smile growing on her face.

"Whatcha thinkin' about?" She asked playfully, drawing out her southern accent.

"Just all of this—I mean, how did you, I just—It's all insane," Creigh finally managed to say.

"I told you; I know what I'm doing. You trusted me and I'm going to take care of you. Don't worry." But a part of Creigh was worried, not that Karen's plan would fail or that he couldn't trust her to take care of them, but that all of what they were doing was going to catch up to them faster than he expected.

After a couple of unnecessary sharp turns, ignoring every stop sign and a few horn honks, they arrived at the bank. Island people drive much differently than drivers in Florida. Regardless, they were now at the bank. It was a much more modern building than the other nearby structures.

Karen jumped out of the stretch SUV and directed everyone else to remain in the vehicles. She quickly disappeared into the bank. One of the two security guards stepped out of the vehicle and placed his back to the concrete wall of the bank. He began rotating his head in a manner where he could see and address any type of danger from all sides. The other security guard remained in the vehicle but was certainly conscious of everything in the nearby surroundings. Street vendors, tourists, and other locals were curiously staring at the stretch SUVs. This made all the boys even more nervous.

After a few minutes, Karen poked her head out the bank doors and motioned for everyone to come inside. It seemed like she was gone for hours but it was really only a few minutes. One by one, the boys filed out of the vehicles with their gym bags tightly gripped. Creigh was carrying his gym bag and Karen's gym bag. The sidewalk bystanders were guessing their identities—*Maybe a basketball team? Nah, too short. Maybe a soccer team? Nah, not enough players and only one player of color.* The growing sidewalk peanut gallery finally concluded that they were a tennis team. Man, were they wrong.

The boys were quickly herded into a large conference room through an eight-foot steel double door. In the center of the room was a beautiful, hand-carved mahogany table. The table seated sixteen people comfortably and was covered with cookies, cupcakes, and soft drinks. The Hammerheads were politely directed to sit down, make themselves comfortable, and feel free to enjoy the goodies. One would have thought the boys would have not had an appetite after eating all the snacks on the ferry ride. Instead, they ate like it was their last meal.

Soon, all but one of the remaining seats were filled with higherups from the bank. One of the security guards was positioned in the corner of the conference room facing the steel doors and the other was just outside the steel doors. The boys were now warming up to the idea of more security and were glad Karen arranged for the security service.

Both parties were exchanging pleasantries and eating goodies at the table. Creigh and the boys were unsure of the Saint John greeting custom, so they just went with the flow. If the person greeted them with a hug, they returned with a hug. If the person greeted them with a kiss on the cheek, they responded with a kiss on the cheek. It was awkward but seemed to satisfy everyone in the room.

As everyone was settling in, the big steel doors opened outward as if royalty were about to enter the room. A very distinguished man entered dressed in a full three-piece suit, pink pocket ascot included. It was obvious that he was the head honcho at the bank. The chair at the end of the table was taller and much nicer than the other chairs. It had mahi-mahi dolphinfish carved into the backrest and armrest. It was obvious this was his chair.

Unfortunately for him, John-Boy was sitting in the chair. The distinguished man walked over to his personal chair, or one might say *throne*, and gave John-Boy a serious but appropriate look. John-Boy continued to look straight ahead, chowing on some fresh cookies, and drinking the sweet fruit juices. John-Boy was in another world. He had obviously taken some pain killers or found some pot before the meeting and was more zoned out than usual.

Creigh got up from his seat and walked over to John-Boy. He leaned over the back of the beautiful chair and half-whispered in John-Boy's ear.

"Get your ass up and move to the vacant seat."

Everyone heard Creigh but did not say a word. John-Boy, his mouth stuffed with cookies, shrugged, and reluctantly hobbled over to the empty seat as if he had done nothing wrong. By now, the boys were whispering among themselves that the last man to enter the room was definitely the one in charge. It was at this point that they secretly declared his new name as "Head Honcho."

The distinguished man sat in his colorful seat and quickly winked at Creigh as if to acknowledge his kind gesture. Creigh nodded back and returned to his seat.

Head Honcho began motioning for everyone to quiet down. He then welcomed all the boys to Saint John. All his staff members clapped on cue. He acknowledged Karen's presence and told the young men how he had met with Karen and Karen's father in this very room on many occasions. This was an effort to make the boys feel more comfortable with him and his foreign bank. It worked.

"What can I do for you today?" he asked.

Before anyone could respond, Creigh jumped in and said, "We would like to deposit some money into our accounts."

Head Honcho nodded and replied, "I assume you all have accounts here."

Creigh looked to Karen, and she quickly nodded her head indicating "yes."

"How much money would you like to deposit in each account?" asked Head Honcho.

Karen looked at Creigh. She still did not know how much money they had. She was guessing it was ten grand or maybe as much as twenty grand.

Creigh looked at Karen and smiled. He then turned to Head Honcho.

"We inherited a lot of money. Can you ensure us that our money is safe here?" asked Creigh.

Head Honcho dropped a few names of rich American people that kept their money in his bank. The boys were familiar with most of the names through politics, the oil business, and news stories.

Karen was embarrassed at this point. Creigh was questioning a man that managed millions of dollars. She was jotting down notes on her pad of paper but took the time to cut her eyes at Creigh in disgust. Creigh was surprised because she rarely, if ever, had done this to him.

"We inherited a little north of $5 million," said Creigh.

Karen's jaw dropped along with her pen. She was staring at Creigh in disbelief. Creigh continued to look at Head Honcho but could sense Karen looking at him.

"We want the accounts to be set up with a debit card and personal checks," said Creigh.

Debit cards were fairly new but would be very useful for the boys.

"Where is the money?" questioned Head Honcho.

In unison and very proudly, the boys flopped their gym bags onto the mahogany table.

This drew an expression of disbelief from everyone seated around the table except the Hammerheads.

Creigh was somewhat prepared for this moment. He took a deep breath, exhaled, and proceeded with his presentation.

"Each gym bag is filled with American currency-sized brown shrink-wrapped packages." Creigh paused to verify that everyone understood him. All the bank employees nodded in concurrence. Karen's jaw was still dropped. Creigh continued. "Each brown shrink-wrapped package contains 250 hundred-dollar bills—or $25,000. Is everyone with me so far?" Creigh asked.

All the bank employees nodded. Karen's jaw was still on the floor.

Creigh continued. "Each gym bag contains just over 200 brown shrink-wrapped packages. Please remove exactly 200 of the packages—$5 million—from each gym bag and deposit the money into the account of the owner of that gym bag. The remaining brown shrink-wrapped packages in the gym bag are the responsibility of the gym bag owner. Does everyone understand?"

All the bank employees nodded in agreement.

Head Honcho continued to act professional but deep down he was delighted beyond belief. His initial thought was $5 million total. He now realized it was $5 million from each new bank customer! He gave a couple of simple hand signals to the bank employees. In response, the bank employees each chose a Hammerhead to their immediate left, introduced themselves and whisked them off to private offices. Each Hammerhead gripped their gym bag tightly and looked to Creigh for concurrence.

Creigh nodded his head and whispered, "It's ok, go with them. They are here to help."

Karen and Creigh remained in the room with Head Honcho and the remaining bank employees. Karen asked for a glass of water. Sweat was beading-up on her beautiful face. Karen's mind was racing.

It was not a few thousand dollars.

It was not $10,000.

It was not $20,000.

It was not $5 million.

It was over $40 million dollars!!

She could not, nor would not, look at Creigh. Was he a criminal? Was he a drug dealer? Karen desperately wanted to ask Creigh questions about how they fell into this money but decided it was not the place nor time. Besides, her daddy's motto was: "We do not discriminate on who can and cannot open a bank account in Saint John."

The bank employees, after permission, opened Creigh and Karen's gym bags and quietly started counting their money. Most banks have bill counting machines, but for whatever reason, they counted the money by hand.

Head Honcho quietly sat in his chair, overseeing the process. He desperately wanted to ask questions about how Creigh and Karen obtained this enormous amount of money but decided it was not the place nor time.

After about thirty minutes, the Hammerheads trickled, one by one, back into the conference room. Each one had a box of checks and two debit cards, which were all connected to their new bank accounts. Karen had set this up in advance of their arrival.

Creigh and Karen were the last to receive their checks and debit cards. Creigh had to remind Karen that she received an equal share as well. Again, she was completely floored.

Head Honcho explained to the group how the debit cards could be used, and safeguards associated with the cards and checks.

To no one's surprise, John-Boy was eating the remaining goodies and certainly not paying attention to Head Honcho. Creigh rolled his eyes and shook his head at John-Boy. Karen saw this and smiled at Creigh. This was the first positive reaction Creigh had seen from Karen in quite some time. This made Creigh feel better.

As they were leaving, each member of the bank team lined up by the door and kissed and hugged each member of the Hammerhead Gang. *This must have been a custom*, they all thought.

Creigh and Karen were the last to leave. After Karen hugged and kissed Head Honcho, she paused and stared him in the eyes.

"I am a grown woman, and this business deal has nothing to do with my father. I would like to keep it that way," Karen said sternly.

Head Honcho squeezed her hand tight and said, "Agreed. You have my word, Miss Karen."

Karen smiled and nodded her head in satisfaction. Creigh overheard this conversation and acknowledged Karen and Head Honcho.

27

DAY 1 IN PARADISE

Despite having walked through the same door only an hour before, Creigh felt different as he walked out of the bank. The weighted pressure of everything falling apart seemed to be lifted. Creigh knew they weren't completely out of the woods, but having the money secure in the bank and being very far away from the farm seemed to give Creigh a slight reprieve from his constant anxiety.

The Hammerheads were all now officially millionaires. Gym bags in hand, they exited the bank building to find their loyal security guards and their stretch SUVs parked directly in front of the bank. Karen and Creigh made a successful effort to not get in the same vehicle as John-Boy and Willy. They knew John-Boy and Willy wanted to go straight to the ferryboat, subsequently hop on a plane and return home to Florida—immediately, if not sooner. Creigh and Karen had other plans for the Hammerheads.

Surprisingly, and at first, the Gang was not as rowdy as anticipated. It had not really sunk in. In both cars, they spoke softly and cautiously about what they were going to do with their money. Their conversations became louder, and their money spending plans grew larger. It went from buying new tennis shoes, to buying motorcycles, to buying boats, to buying yachts, to buying mansions. The boys were so caught up in their spending dreams that they did not notice that the stretch SUVs drove right past the ferryboat landing.

They rode through the narrow streets of Saint John, before the main city faded away and they were surrounded by thick, lush trees on one side of the SUV and the ocean on the other. Creigh watched the ocean waves crashing against the white, sandy beaches and found himself daydreaming about sinking his bare toes into it and letting the ocean wash away the last of his anxiety.

Sooner than later, the SUVs turned onto what appeared to be a private drive. The boys were now aware of the scenery change and were somewhat confused. Was this the part where the handsome bodyguards murder them and take all their money? This is more than the boys bargained for, especially John-Boy and Willy. They were "assured" that they would be going straight from the bank to the airport and back to Florida. This was not happening, and they were not happy.

The SUVs eventually came to a stop at a massive set of iron gates. There were large metal carvings of a Hammerhead shark on each gate. The carvings were beautiful and there was no doubt they were very expensive.

The boys that were in Karen's SUV could not help but notice Karen franticly digging through her oversized purse. Like most women, she had everything but the kitchen sink in her purse. Finally, they could see the look of relief on her face as she pulled out a remote-control key fob. Karen pressed the button on the remote and the massive iron gates slowly opened. The stretch SUVs entered the compound and the iron gates closed behind them.

Most of the Gang were curious and excited, but cautious at the same time. John-Boy and Willy were not part of the curious and excited group. They were not happy at all and were very vocal about their current situation. This was not the road to the ferryboat and certainly was not the airport. Of course, their complaints fell on deaf ears as Creigh and Karen were purposely not in their vehicle.

The vehicles traversed slightly upward on the winding road. By now, the terrain was open enough that the boys had a view of what was known as Cruz Bay. There were many small boats and a surprising number of large yachts motoring about in the bay. Beautiful mansions speckled the hill side. The scenery was simply breathtaking.

The winding driveway soon came to an end. The drivers' shutdown the SUVs and, as always, quickly opened the passenger doors for the young men. The boys exited the vehicles and stared in amazement. In front of them was the biggest, most beautiful mansion they had ever seen. It was like something from a movie. The house was at least four stories tall. It was a Mediterranean-style home with a clay tile roof. In their view, they could see an infinity pool on the third level. There was a tennis court, which also doubled as a basketball court on the second floor. Down the mountainside was a private dock extending into Cruz Bay. The dock was secured with iron gates very similar to the gates at the entrance to the compound. Several boats and jet skis were moored to the dock. One would only assume these were private vessels that belonged to the owner of this mansion.

John-Boy and Willy were still angry but speechless as well. Why were they here?

Karen quickly got out in front of the group and addressed them accordingly. "Welcome to the Shark Cave...a 10,000 square foot vacation home here in Saint John. Because you deserve it, Creigh and I reserved this place for the next seven days. It has ten bedrooms, twelve bathrooms, two pools, a tennis court, and a fleet of water vessels for your pleasure. The house is stocked with food, booze and, yes, John-Boy, there might be a bag or two of weed on the premises as well." Karen added. "It has a fully stocked kitchen as well as an outdoor kitchen. So...who can cook?" Karen laughed.

"Actually, Creigh's not so bad," John-Boy offered, having lived with him the last year.

"No worries, I've hired a private chef. You boys just relax."

"This is all so incredible! Thank you!" Creigh said, taking Karen into his arms.

The boys laughed about the weed comment and, John-Boy, still very sore, even cracked a smile. All the young men were stunned at their new living quarters. The name, Shark Cave, was super cool and fitting for the Hammerhead Gang.

Creigh tipped the limo drivers and the bodyguards. They were very gracious for the large tips and let Creigh know they were available 24/7. They departed the compound but assured Creigh they were only a phone call away.

Karen unlocked the front door and motioned for the Gang to enter. As the boys made their way into the house, it was evident that the inside of the house was more impressive than the outside. There were several paintings of sharks hanging from the walls and even a head mount of a Hammerhead shark in the living room. The Shark Cave was a perfect match for these guys.

"There are two kitchens, four refrigerators, a walk-in freezer, a commercial grilling station, an elevator and much, much more," said Karen. The boys were in awe.

Karen continued with her presentation. "Your Master Suites are labeled with your name on the bedroom door. Each one of you has a bedroom and bathroom that is solely yours. Willy and John-Boy, your Master Suites are on the second floor. Y'all have a game room on your floor as well."

Both Willy and John-Boy were still trying to act grumpy about their extended stay in Saint John but could not hold back smiles as she described their living arrangements.

"Danny, Terrance and Nicholas, your Master Suites are on the third floor. Y'all have a super cool infinity pool outside your bedrooms," said Karen.

Danny and Nicholas's faces lit up with excitement. Terrance had a puzzled, sour look on his face.

"Not that it matters, but where is your room?" asked Terrance in a somewhat sarcastic tone.

"Creigh and I are sharing a room on the fourth floor. Each of you have your own room," answered Karen. She decided to remain tight-lipped in describing the fourth floor. After all, it was the penthouse and had its own pool, hot tub, game room, and sauna.

"One more thing before you inspect your rooms," said Karen. She took a deep breath and continued. "Creigh secretly checked your shirt, shoe, and trouser sizes before we left the states. I took the liberty of purchasing clothes and toiletries for each of y'all. Your closets and dresser drawers should be filled with new clothes. Your bathrooms have soap, shampoo, and other toiletry needs. We hope you like the island style clothes. It is the least we could do for all of you."

Before Karen could finish her sentence, the boys were headed up the steps to their suites.

The arrangements were even better than Karen had described. Each boy had new sandals, tennis shoes, shorts, underwear, bathing suites, T-shirts, and colorful silk island shirts. It was obvious that Karen chose the clothing styles—not Creigh!

To each Hammerhead, this was more of a fantasy than reality.

The boys were once again in unchartered territory. But for once, the unchartered territory was viewed in a good way.

Creigh shouted so everyone in the house could hear him, "Take a shower, put on something comfortable, and meet on the main floor in thirty minutes."

Creigh and Karen retreated to their penthouse suite. Creigh plopped down onto the king-sized bed with a look of exhaustion. Karen followed Creigh's lead, but she landed directly on top of him. These two had not had any alone time since their passionate meeting in Birmingham. A lot had transpired in the past forty-eight hours and these two needed to have a conversation. A couple of quick pecks on the lips led to a longer, sexier kiss which led to the removal of all clothes which led to a quick love-making session. So much for the needed conversation.

Along with everyone else, Creigh and Karen showered and changed into some of their new clothes. Karen brought clothes from the states but also ordered new clothes during the Hammerhead shopping spree. "What is one more suitcase?" she thought.

After about thirty minutes, all the Hammerheads except Creigh and Karen were gathered in the main living room. Creigh and Karen were tardy due to their rumble in the hay and the simple fact that women take longer to get dolled-up. Their tardiness did not matter because the boys were busy looking in closets, pressing buttons, and munching on snacks from the grocery store sized pantry.

After another thirty minutes had passed, Terrance yelled up the staircase, "We are leaving!!"

Karen and Creigh snickered because they knew that was impossible. The boys did not know where to go.

Within a minute or two, Creigh clopped down the staircase wearing his new sandals and joined the boys in the main living room. They all picked fun at each other's island shirts and shorts. Willy had on a straw hat that was perfect for island life.

"Willy?" Creigh motioned to the straw hat on his head. "What's that?"

"Found it in the closet, last renter musta' left it there."

"It looks good on you."

Willy nodded in equal approval.

The boys all turned at the sound of a ding coming from behind them. They gawked as the metal door slid open to reveal Karen standing in the center of the elevator.

"No shit, this place has an elevator?!" Danny gasped.

"Yep, just in case your legs get tired," Karen winked.

The boys thought the elevator was the coolest thing they had ever seen in a house, besides the head mount of the Hammerhead shark.

Creigh reached his hand out for Karen, wanting her as close to him as possible. She was gorgeous in her skimpy, yellow island dress that reached just under her butt. Her sandals laced up her calves just really sent Creigh's thoughts reeling about taking her back up to the bedroom and leaving the Gang to fend for themselves.

"All right boys, let's saddle up, we are going out!" Karen announced.

Before going any further, Creigh decided this was the time to address the Gang concerning safety and livelihood. He had been planning this brief but important "talk" ever since they left the Hooker Farm for the last time.

"Wait, wait, before we go, we need to talk about some rules," Creigh interjected.

Creigh blocked the front door from the rest of the Gang. He turned and faced them while raising his right hand in the air.

"Let me have your attention for a quick minute," said Creigh.

There were a few groans and cackles but that was always to be expected from this group.

"Congratulations. You are all millionaires," said Creigh. All the boys clapped and made dog barking noises in unison.

He then made eye contact with each Hammerhead. He continued. "But do not act like millionaires. Be humble."

He paused in between each sentence in hope that his words would sink in. "There are good people everywhere. Unfortunately, there are bad people everywhere too...Be conscious of your actions and surroundings...Keep an eye on each other...Let everyone know where you are going and what you are doing...Communicate...Got it?"

All the boys nodded in agreement.

"I love you guys and would take a sword for you," said Creigh. He repeated this to each member as he went around the room embracing them.

This brought tears to Karen's eyes. She now truly realized the bond these guys shared.

"OK. The millionaire speech is over...And remember, you took an oath of secrecy...Now, let the games begin!" shouted Creigh.

This was a term the boys used every time they were about to partake in a new adventure. Creigh's declaration was followed by more dog woofing from the boys.

Karen wiped her teary eyes and motioned for everyone to follow her. She made her way through an unfamiliar (to the boys) area of the house and out a side door. There was a neatly carved walking path leaving the house and headed down the hillside. With Karen in the lead, the Gang marched down the path. Willy and Danny helped John-Boy limp along. There were small trees and jungle-like bushes on each side of the path. The view of Cruz Bay was partially blocked but still beautiful. After about 300 yards, the path dumped into a sandy white beach.

The boys all stopped and stared at what was in front of them. There was an island style building perched right in the middle of the beach. There was reggae music playing, people dancing, and a full-service bar & restaurant. This was the first sign of fun the boys had seen since arriving in Saint John—and boy, was it jumpin'. The boys had hit a homerun! It was like their own private bar attached to the Shark Cave! They would soon find out they were at the world-famous Beach Bar Saint John. It was the most happening place to be on the island. Creigh took note that there was a nice mixture of locals and tourists. He could tell the tourists by their dress and skin. The locals had rougher, darker skin, tanned by being in the sun most of the day. Not to mention, they wore their button-down shirts open to reveal their chests. The tourists had Oxford shirts, gold watches on their wrists, and aviator sunglasses. They were clearly very rich and not from the island. It did not go unnoticed by Creigh that he and the Gang looked just like a tourist.

As they were walking up to the bar, Danny asked the Gang if the "Radius Rule" was in effect? All the boys grinned and agreed that the "Radius Rule' was in effect. Karen was oblivious to what they were talking about and turned to Creigh for guidance.

"What are they talking about?" asked Karen.

Creigh smiled at her and said, "It's a guy-thing."

Karen did not like that answer and gave Creigh a hands-on-the-hips look.

"It doesn't apply to you and me, baby," said Creigh.

"Well, then what is it?" asked Karen.

Creigh sighed and said, "I will tell you later. The Radius Rule will never ever apply to you and me. Let's just have fun right now."

Karen was semi-satisfied with that answer...which also meant she was semi-unsatisfied with the answer. Creigh really did not want to tell her about the Radius Rule and later scolded Danny for mentioning it in front of her.

The boys created the Radius Rule when they were in high school. During that time, they all had steady local girlfriends, but they enjoyed partying in Panama City, Destin, Fort Walton, Navarre Beach, and Gulf Shores. The Radius Rule allowed the boys to pretend to be single if they were more than fifty miles (the Radius) from home. It was somewhat of a joke, but the boys still like using the term.

The Hammerhead Gang bellied up to the cool bar and ordered big fruity alcoholic drinks. Creigh and Karen were not interested in the bar scene, so they walked over to the beach and reserved chairs, umbrellas, and beach towels for the entire Gang. Soon, Terrance, Danny, and Nicholas joined Karen and Creigh at the beach. Willy and John-Boy remained at the bar. Creigh figured they were still sulking from not getting their wish to go home. *If they want to act like babies that is fine with me*, he thought.

Terrance, the outdoorsman, spotted a salty old fisherman casting out lines from the beach. The man would walk out in the water, waist-deep, and cast his line as far as possible. He would then walk back to the shore and place the butt end of the rod into a piece of PVC pipe that was secured in the ground. He had five rod-n-reel combos spaced out about thirty feet apart. He would sit in his rusty old chair and watch the rods. When a fish would take the bait, the rod would double over. The ole man would hobble over and reel in the fish. He caught pinfish, mackerel, bluefish, and a couple of other species Terrance did not recognize. Regardless of species, the fish all went into his ice chest.

The old man's methods were very similar to how the boys fished for sharks back in Florida. Terrance struck-up a conversation with him and eventually asked if he would mind letting him reel in a fish or two. The ole man had no intentions of letting this punk kid take over his fishing rods.

However, when Terrance handed the old man a fifty-dollar bill, things changed.

"Ole Cum Get Em!" shouted the ole salty fisherman.

Terrance had no idea what this meant but smiled and shouted, "Ole Cum Get Em!" back to him.

They were now best friends and Terrance could reel in as many fish as he wanted. Terrance spent most of the afternoon baiting hooks, catching fish, dumping them in the ice chest, and then rerigging. The salty ole fisherman realized Terrance knew what he was doing so he, without notice to Terrance, eased up to the bar with his fresh fifty-dollar bill. This was a win-win for both men.

Terrance and the old salty fisherman smiled, laughed, and exchanged several more "Ole Cum Get Ems" throughout the day. Terrance never understood the meaning of "Ole Cum Get Em" but kinda liked the sound of the phrase. He said it to the other Hammerheads and other beach goers. Soon, everyone in Cruz Bay was saying "Ole Cum Get Em!" without knowing its meaning.

Nicholas and Danny swam some, peppered a volleyball back-n-forth, and girl-watched the entire afternoon. Every so often, Terrance would have multiple fishing rods doubled over and would yell for their help. Ole Cum Get Em!!

Danny and Nicholas would jog over and reel in the fish but leave it flopping in the sand. They did not want to be tainted with fish smell while attempting to make time with the ladies. Terrance would have to deal with the flopping fish. Of course, he did not mind doing this at all.

Karen and Creigh sat in their chairs, sipping fruity alcoholic drinks while watching Nicholas, Terrance, and Danny. A beautiful waitress wearing an outfit that left little for the imagination would trudge out onto the beach and bring the entire crew fresh drinks as needed. She did not mind because the rumors were already circulating Saint John about this group of handsome young men and their generous tips.

"Where are Willy and John-Boy?" asked Karen.

"I guess they're still at the bar," said Creigh.

Karen and Creigh remained seated in their beach lounge chairs but surveyed the beach and bar area. There was no sign of John-Boy and Willy.

Half-jokingly, Creigh said, "They probably went to the airport to try and catch an afternoon flight back to Florida."

"They wouldn't do that, would they?" Karen asked.

Creigh did not respond.

An uneasy feeling came over Creigh. The two renegades just might be on their way back to Florida. Did they not pay attention to his millionaire speech? Surely not.

Creigh and Karen sat on the beach for about another hour. Finally, Creigh had worried enough. He decided to do a quick search of the beach area for the two rebels. Karen appeared to be asleep. He whispered in her ear that he was going to look for Willy and John-Boy and then gave her a kiss on the cheek. She incoherently mumbled something back at him as he walked toward the bar.

"Hey man, you seen those other guys we came down with?" Creigh asked the bartender.

"They left a while ago with 'dem girls and didn't pay 'der tab neither," said the bartender as he motioned back up to the house.

Creigh rolled his eyes and sighed out loud. The bartender was not expecting Creigh to pay their tab. He enjoyed talking with Willy and John-Boy and assumed they would return to pay their bill.

Without further ado, Creigh thanked the bartender, handed him $200 and headed up the path. The bartender was elated. He rang the "tip bell" loud and long. This let everyone know that a patron had just left a very generous tip. So much for not acting like millionaires.

When Creigh arrived at the Shark Cave, he could see that the front door was ajar and one of the garage doors was open. This concerned him and he proceeded into the house with caution.

He could hear loud music coming from the second floor. The smell of burning marijuana was overwhelming.

Creigh made his way to the second floor and could hear laughing, giggling, and music coming from the first bedroom. This was John-Boy's room, and the door was cracked open.

Creigh pushed the door fully open and entered the room.

Creigh was accustomed to John-Boy's antics, but this was off-the-charts. There were four girls lying in the oversized king bed with Willy and John-Boy. They were island girls and only wearing thong panties. They were young, quite curvy, and very beautiful.

John-Boy and Willy were clad only in underwear—it was the new underwear Creigh and Karen had bought for them. Their eyes were half closed, and they were both giggling like little schoolgirls. It was obvious that the six of them were high on recreational drugs.

"Duuuude, don't you ever knock?" piped John-Boy.

Creigh glared at the six of them without saying a word. Part of him wanted to send the girls packing and then strangle Willy and John-Boy.

However, John-Boy and Willy had been angry, vocal, and pestering everyone about going home. They were now happy and in a good place.

Creigh cracked a big smile and said, "Ladies, can I have a moment with my friends, Willy and John-Boy? Please help yourself to any of the food and drinks in the kitchen."

The girls promptly got out of the bed and headed for the kitchen. Each one of them gave Creigh "the eye" as they walked past him. He smiled at them but already knew where "his bread was buttered." These girls had nothing on Karen.

John-Boy rolled over in the bed and turned his back to Creigh.

He could care less about what Creigh had to say. He was gonna walk his own walk, and talk his own talk, no matter what.

Willy was quite different. Creigh was his best friend and brought him into the Hammerhead Gang. He respected Creigh and would do anything Creigh asked him to do. After all, he would still be living in the streets if it were not for Creigh.

Creigh sat on the corner of the bed and smiled at Willy and John-Boy.

"I am glad you both are having fun. We are all having fun at the beach as well," said Creigh.

John-Boy and Willy were shocked. They thought a butt-chewing was on the menu. Instead, Creigh sounded kind and caring.

Creigh continued, "All I ask as that you remember the millionaire speech I gave earlier. Most of our money is in the Trustworthy Saint John Bank but each of us has a gym bag in the house with over $100,000 in it. If you invite the wrong person or people into the house, they could rob you or us of all our cash."

Willy and John-Boy had not thought about this scenario. They perked up immediately and became concerned about where the four beauties were. Willy opened the door and peeked over the balcony. He could see all the girls sitting comfortably in the living room. He then looked in his closet and could see his gym bag was zipped tight and remained in the same place he stowed it. He sighed in relief.

"They could steal your blank bank checks and debit card," said Creigh.

Creigh paused and allowed this to sink in. For once, it seemed like John-Boy was listening and would try to comply. He rolled over in the bed and slowly nodded his head in agreement to Creigh.

"Have fun but please be careful...for all of our sakes," said Creigh.

With that, he left the room. Willy and John-Boy were shocked that this was the end of the speech.

"IGYB Forever!" yelled Willy.

Creigh continued walking away from John-Boy and Willy but pointed his finger back at Willy and said, "Back at ya, buddy!"

Creigh skipped down the stairs and walked past the girls. By now, they had covered themselves with beach towels and throw-blankets.

Creigh laughed and said, "They are all yours. Have fun."

The girls made their way back up the steps and into the bedroom with Willy and John-Boy.

Creigh returned to the beach with Karen.

Terrance caught fish 'til dark.

Nicholas and Danny met a couple of hotties from Atlanta, GA. They were sharing drinks and stories at the bar.

All was good with the Hammerhead Gang in Saint John.

Ole Cum Get Em!

28

A KILLER BEHIND BARS TONIGHT

For a moment, when Creigh opened his eyes in the morning with the sun cascading through the open room, he forgot where he was and what had happened in the last forty-eight hours. The first sign that he wasn't still in Milton, Florida, in his twin bed in the place he lived with John-Boy, was the smell of Karen. A mixture of coconut and sunscreen. He reached over and touched Karen, making sure she was real. She moaned and curled into his bare chest. Creigh gazed at the ceiling, trying to wrap his mind around the fact that this was his new life.

An hour later, Creigh padded down to the kitchen to make some coffee only to find that Nicholas was already there, as well as Terrence pouring his first cup of coffee. He made sure to grab his own cup before addressing the boys.

"Mornin'," Creigh finally offered after his first sip. "How ya' feelin'?"

"I'm fine," Nicholas smiled, having gone to bed early last night. "As for the others," he shrugged, chuckling to himself.

"Yeah, I figure they might be hurtin' today after that party last night."

John-Boy and Willy's party had lasted well into the early hours of the morning. Karen had been nice to cook everyone a big pot of jambalaya which hit the spot for everyone. The dinner had been served around the large patio table, and Creigh had gotten to know the girls that the boys brought back, and they weren't that bad. Karen and Creigh had even partied a few hours last night but had called it much earlier.

"I think the party didn't die until about four in the morning," Terrence said. "Pretty sure the girls are still here too."

"Well, that's just great," Creigh rolled his eyes, annoyed that John-Boy and Willy didn't seem to understand the danger of keeping random girls in the house.

"Mornin'," Karen said as she strolled into the kitchen in only her flowered robe.

"So, what happens when our week runs out here?" Nicholas asked, looking directly at Karen who had clearly been in charge of all this.

"Well," Karen shrugged, giving Creigh a side glance. "Whatever you want, I guess."

"Anything but go home, right?" Nicholas asked, looking at Creigh.

"It's just not safe, man," Creigh offered. "At least not right now. I'm not sayin' never go back, but for right now we just need to lay low."

"Let's just enjoy the week," Karen interjected. "I've got a lot planned for us."

"Like what?"

She gave them a pointed look. "Like don't get too drunk today because we are going out tonight."

Creigh shrugged when Nicholas and Terrence looked to him for answers.

The day passed tortuously slow for Creigh as he was anxious for the evening news to verify that Kent Poole had been arrested. They'd all tried to distract themselves by playing volleyball on the beach, drinking fruity drinks from the bar, and fishing with the old fisherman who was still out on the beach, but nothing seemed to quell Creigh's anxiety. Not today.

At exactly five o'clock the entire Gang was sitting on the couch staring at the national news report. It cycled through a few stories, then Creigh's heart stopped. There he was. A picture of Kent was blasted on the screen, right next to Deputy Delay.

"An anonymous tip brings a serial killer to justice tonight in Jackson, Mississippi. Believed to be the killer behind multiple missing children, Kent Poole has been taken into custody at the Hinds County Jail. This arrest comes after a Deputy, by the name of Joshua Delay, reported to the local FBI that he had information on the death of the girl in Destin, Florida just a few months ago. This is an ongoing investigation—"

"Hey!" Terrence shouted as the television went black.

"That's enough," Creigh announced. "That bastard is behind bars tonight, let's celebrate!"

Finally, the elephant-sized weight on his chest had been lifted. Kent was arrested. It made national news, so there was no way he was getting out of this one. No way.

29

DAY 2, 3 AND 4 IN PARADISE

For the next three days, the Gang lived in paradise as if they were on Spring Break vacation. Starting around noon, Karen and Creigh moved from coffee in bed to sipping fruity alcohol drinks on the beach. Like clockwork, each day they would return to the Shark Cave around 3 p.m. for a nap...and an intimate roll in the hay. The rest of the Gang would catcall at Creigh and Karen as they headed to the house. The boys knew what was going on. Creigh and Karen were usually tipsy and were not concerned with the boys and their taunts.

Danny and Nicholas invited Terrance to join them, playing on the beach. This trio met a mixture of local and touristy girls. In return, Terrance rented a midsized center console boat and took Danny and Nicholas offshore fishing. They caught mackerel, black fin tuna, and a wahoo. Terrance cleaned the catch and made an incredibly tasty ceviche-style fish dip. One night, he surprised everyone by frying and grilling fish for the entire Gang. The fresh fish were delicious, and everyone was impressed with Terrance's culinary skills.

And then there was John-Boy and Willy. By now, the swelling in John-Boy's eye had gone down but he still had a nice shiner. His collar bone appeared to be fractured but remained in place. Creigh recalled reading a medical journal about broken collar bones and that there was not much that could be done about them from a medical standpoint...except keep the arm immobilized and the patient filled with pain killers. John-Boy had the pain killer part mastered. Every night, there was loud music and laughter from the second-floor suites. Each morning around 11 a.m., they would emerge from their rooms and stagger into the kitchen, looking for food and coffee. It seemed like they had a different girl, or girls, every night. These were the same two guys that wanted to return to Florida on day one.

On the afternoon of day four, Creigh, Terrance, Danny, and Nicholas were hanging out at the world-famous Beach Bar Saint John, playing bar games such as Hook on a Ring, Cornhole, and Darts. They befriended the owner of the Beach Bar, Reed, and soon he was partaking in tequila shots with the boys.

Karen decided to take a day off from the beach "routine" and go shopping. After all, a girl can never have enough clothes, right?

Oddly enough, Willy and John-Boy had not been seen nor heard all day.

By 5 p.m., Karen, shopping bags in hand, made her way to the Beach Bar Saint John to find four sloshed young men—five, counting Reed, the owner of the Beach Bar. The boys and Reed were singing karaoke. There was no other way to describe their performance but horrific. They sounded like a pack of hound dogs chasing a fox through an Alabama swamp. The crowd was laughing and booing in an attempt to shame these guys off the stage. It did not work. It only made them sing louder! Creigh finally saw Karen and motioned for her to come up on stage. Unlike most girls, Karen embraced the situation. She ordered herself a double shot of whiskey, threw it back, and then joined the new Saint John singing group on stage. Unfortunately, Karen's singing was just as bad as the others, but she was much easier for the crowd to look at as she belted out *Friends In Low Places*. It was a big hit!

Still, there was no sign of John-Boy and Willy. Had they had enough and gone back to Florida? This did not seem likely due to the large time they were having each night. Were they in trouble or possibly in jail? Maybe...If so, they probably deserved it.

It was now 10 p.m. Terrance, Danny, and Nicholas were paired up with three island girls and did not have a care in the world. Creigh and Karen were becoming somewhat concerned with the disappearance of Willy and John-Boy. Reed, the bar owner and new friend, contacted the VI Police Department. There were no reports nor incidents with the names Willy and John-Boy.

At about 11 p.m., three men entered the Beach Bar. Two of them looked very familiar (John-Boy and Willy). The third man was a local named James. James frequented the Beach Bar from time-to-time. Reed shook his head in disgust. James was not a good person. He was known as a shyster in the Cruz Bay community. He often left his bar tab unpaid and was known to embezzle money from tourists.

Trying not to sound mad, even though he was very angry, Creigh asked, "Where have y'all been?"

"Our new friend, James, took us on a personal tour of Cruz Bay," said Willy.

This seemed peculiar. Willy and John-Boy were not typical tourists, and James was certainly not a typical tour guide.

"You guys have been gone for over twelve hours! Cruz Bay is not that big!" exclaimed Creigh.

There was an awkward period of silence. Something was not right with this situation. Finally, Willy broke the silence.

"We were looking at houses and condos...permanent places to live," said Willy.

Again, there was a long silence. Finally, John-Boy and Willy glanced at one another and started laughing.

"Ok. We like it here so much we plan to stay here...permanently. We have no intentions of returning to the United States," said Willy.

Willy nor John-Boy realized that the Virgin Islands were part of the United States but that really did not matter at this point.

Karen finally broke the awkward silence by congratulating and hugging John-Boy and Willy.

"Did y'all find a house?" asked Karen.

"No, but James showed a couple of his houses, and they were affordable," said Willy.

Immediately, Reed jumped into the conversation.

"Whoa, whoa, whoa!" exclaimed Reed. "Did you guys give James any money?"

John-Boy, whom had been silent this entire time, piped in. "Not that it is any of your business, but yes, we gave him a down payment."

"How much?" asked Reed.

"None of your damn business!" growled John-Boy.

Reed looked to Willy for the answer.

"Five thousand each," said Willy.

By now, Reed was boiling-mad. He had dealt with James on many occasions and this took the cake. "You do know James is not a real estate agent and certainly not a homeowner, right?" Reed asked.

Before John-Boy or Willy could answer, Reed continued. "James is a well-known local crook and has spent more days behind bars than days walking freely. He preys on dumbass tourists like you guys."

Willy, although not happy with Reed's description of him and John-Boy, turned to James and asked, "Is this true?"

James absolutely denied any wrongdoing and, at the same time, was slowly back peddling away from the group. He suddenly turned and made a run for it. Unfortunately for James, he chose the wrong person to shyster. Before he could make it ten meters, Willy pounced on James's back and flattened him to the white sandy beach. James was an older and slighter man. It looked as if Willy's takedown was very, very painful.

Willy grabbed a banded stack of money from each of James's front pockets. It was obviously some of the reward money from the Hooker Farm. He tossed one banded stack of hundred-dollar bills to John-Boy. He removed one of those bills from his stack before putting the stack securely in his pocket. He stuffed the bill in James's front pocket. James was still agonizing from the brutal takedown.

"Here. This is for your trouble," said Willy.

James laid there motionless as the Gang departed. Soon, a couple of bar patrons helped James up from the beautiful white sandy beach and into a seat at the bar. He was wincing, but now had $100 to drink-off his pain. He ordered a beer and scanned the bar for his potential next victim.

The group remained silent as they walked the winding trail back to the Shark Cave. Reality had set in. The money was great...but trouble also came with it. As they entered the house, Creigh reminded Willy and John-Boy of his millionaire speech. His words fell on deaf ears.

Willy and John-Boy peeled off to the second floor and Creigh trotted up the stairs to the penthouse suite. The third floor was silent as Danny, Terrance, and Nicholas were still out on the town.

Before retiring to the penthouse, Karen softly tapped on Willy's door. Willy opened the door and was surprised to see Karen. John-Boy was also in Willy's room and had just lit up a funny cigarette.

"Come in," said Willy.

Karen entered the room and sat on the bed beside John-Boy. He offered her a puff of his joint and, surprisingly, she took it. This made John-Boy crack a smile.

"I am happy about you guys moving here and I want to help you. My father's bank has a real estate office. With your permission, I will meet with the on-duty agent in the morning and line-up some houses for viewing tomorrow afternoon. How does that sound?" said Karen.

Willy and John-Boy were genuinely excited after hearing this.

"What are you looking for? And what area?" asked Karen.

Willy and John-Boy told Karen of the pseudo houses James showed them. She was familiar with the houses and knew that they were in a very bad area. The poorest of the poor lived in this area. Willy and John-Boy were clueless about real estate.

"What is your price range?" asked Karen.

"$200,000 is what we were going to pay James," said John-Boy.

Karen could not help but think badly about James the shyster. He was going to take $200,000 from these guys and give them a $30,000 house in the slave labor area in Cruz Bay. Luckily, this did not come to fruition.

"Alrighty. Let's plan to look at houses tomorrow afternoon. Meet me here at the Shark Cave at 2 p.m.," said Karen.

"Cool," John-Boy answered.

John-Boy and Willy were happy they replaced James with beautiful Karen.

She ran up the stairs to join Creigh in their room.

Creigh was laying flat on the bed, his head starting to slightly spin from all the shots that Reed had fed them at the bar. Suddenly, Karen's face came into view. He smiled, pulling her in and kissing her. She rolled over next to him and cuddled up on his chest.

"What do you think about Willy staying on the island?" she asked.

"I mean, I think he deserves whatever he wants. After the shit he's been through and how he helped us," Creigh didn't finish his words. He consciously did not want to make Karen complicit in what Willy and he had to do at the cemetery.

"I think you deserve it too." Karen perched up on her arm so Creigh could look her in the eyes. "What do you want?"

"I want you." He smiled, kissing her again.

"But what kind of life do you want? Do you want to have a life here? Do you want a life back home?"

"I want a life with you," Creigh admitted. He'd thought about it, at length, how much he wanted to have a life with Karen. She was it for him—the one.

"I want a life with you too. But is this going to be our life—partyin' and drinkin' all day?"

"No. I thought we were on vacation?"

"Yeah, we are. But in a few days, we have to figure out real-life, next steps."

Creigh thought for a moment about what Karen was asking. What did he want? "Maybe I want to stay here too."

Karen tried to suppress her smile, but she couldn't stop it from growing and taking over her face. "What?"

"I want to stay here too—with you." Creigh smiled. "So...how many houses are we actually going to be looking for tomorrow?"

"I think we can find a place for everyone here. I think this is y'all's new home."

Creigh loved the sound of that, and he loved Karen.

30

TOURIST TO LOCAL

Karen and Creigh were at the bank at 8 a.m. sharp. The bank did not open to the public till 9 a.m. but Karen and the realtor, Ayanna, had agreed to meet earlier. Karen immediately hugged Ayanna's neck, having known her since she was a child. Ayanna's dark hair was pulled back into a bun, with her glasses perched on the edge of her nose, giving her a sophisticated look for her young age, as she looked Creigh up and down.

"Ayanna's been a good friend, a sister of sorts," Karen explained.

"Which means I'll be sizing you up. Making sure you're good enough for my girl." She tapped Creigh on his shoulder in jest.

"I accept the challenge," Creigh laughed.

Ayanna was a beautiful young woman and had worked at the bank for five years. She climbed the ladder very quickly in the bank. She was a hard worker and good looking. This made for a great combination in her business.

Once inside her private office, Karen briefed Ayanna, the bank realtor, of the circumstances. She certainly did not go into detail of how they obtained their wealth but did let her know they were looking for a small house or condo and would be paying with cash.

Ayanna was excited to hear they were paying in cash. This made her job much easier, and she would receive her commission much sooner. She was also excited to meet the Hammerhead Gang because Karen had high standards and really bragged on the looks of these young men. It was a win-win.

"Let me show you some condos I think you all will be impressed with and then we'll look at some houses."

Creigh called the boys and gave them the address of the condos where they would meet. Next, the three piled into Ayanna's BMW convertible to see the properties. All of them had water access, pool access, and were in great locations. *The Gang would love any of them*, Creigh considered. As they pulled up to the first place, Ayanna's eyes widened at the group of handsome men waiting at the entrance.

"Ayanna, meet the Gang," Creigh offered. Each one put their best foot forward to impress Ayanna, which didn't surprise Creigh. After all, she was very good looking.

"Okay, so we are in Chocolate Hole, which is a great location. And this is a beautiful condominium complex called the Westin and does well in the rental market. We are on the south side of the island, which is pretty low-key. Tons of amenities—tennis court, pool, spa, on-site restaurant. It has it all, and the view. You'll be shocked. Oh, and each condo comes with a set of chairs right on the beach." Ayannna guided them through the lobby and after briefly checking in with the concierge, she returned with keys.

"So, each unit is pretty similar, but I will show you a few different on-site locations and views you get. Each unit is a townhome with two bedrooms, each with a private bathroom on the top floor and a full living and kitchen area on the bottom floor. All units are fully furnished, so no need to worry about all that stuff, which is nice."

Ayanna handed Karen and each boy a brochure which provided pictures and details of the entire complex. It was nicer than Creigh imagined, and the location was a bonus. It was just far away enough for the craziness of Cruz Bay but still close enough to get there within thirty minutes for a good time.

"These units are about 1,500 square feet and around 50,000 US dollars," Ayanna explained as she opened the first condo. The Gang were in shock as they walked through the place. The view was stunning!

"Dude, this balcony is sick," said John-Boy. "I'm sold, let's go."

"Okay, just wait, we have a lot to see here," Karen assured.

After viewing four other condos on the Westin property, the Gang followed Ayanna into the heart of Cruz Bay area. There she showed the boys condos that were right on the main street with sweeping views of the vibrating Cruz Bay. It was the complete opposite of the tranquil feel of the Westin, but that was the point. Creigh wanted to show the boys two very different options.

"I mean, I gotta say I like the Westin," Willy said after they'd viewed all the condos. "But being close to town is nice."

"Well, we do still have some homes to consider if you want to go around with Creigh and Karen this afternoon," Ayanna offered.

"Not me," Terrence announced. "I'm sold on the Westin."

"It's a great investment property," Ayanna agreed.

"Yeah, it would be, but I'm not so sure just yet," Terrence admitted.

It was clear to Creigh that the boys liked Saint John Island, but it wouldn't be where they settled, not in the long term. Nicholas wanted to go back to graduate school and was not going to give that up. John-Boy and Willy had nothing back in Pensacola, so it was clear they'd be staying. But Terrence and Danny were wild cards. They could stay or find themselves going somewhere else. Danny's father had died but he still had his mother back home in Milton; he couldn't leave her behind. Terrence had family too. Creigh saw them going back, at least, at some point.

"John-Boy, any thoughts?" Ayanna asked.

"I mean, let's look at some houses."

"All right, so John-Boy and Willy you can squeeze in with us. Boys," she turned to the others. "I guess we'll see you all later tonight."

"What's tonight?" Terrence asked, looking at Creigh.

"Boys, we are getting at the end of our run here, so just a special dinner tonight. Be ready and don't go back and get drunk today," Creigh jeered.

"Yeah, yeah, we got you." Terrence, Danny, and Nicholas piled back in the SUV to ride back to the house, while John-Boy, Willy, Creigh, and Karen really did squeeze into Ayanna's suddenly very tiny convertible to drive up the mountain to see some houses.

Ayanna twisted the car up the mountain through the trees and barely saw the road that cut through the thickest part of the woods. Ayanna slowed the car to a stop at a small iron gate that had an oversized iguana attached to the front. After unlocking the gate, she pulled the car deeper into the woods.

"All right, we are in the heart of the jungle. Very private and picturesque. You are surrounded by the lush forest and this property stretches for miles, so you are uber isolated up here." John-Boy glared at Creigh, knowing he had been the one to tell Ayanna he needed privacy. "Outdoor grill and pool in the back. Garden over there. And this place is listed at $563,000, but I think we can get it slightly lower due to the fact it's been on the market for a minute."

"It's not bad," Willy offered, but Creigh could tell their faces didn't like it.

"Let's keep going," Creigh announced.

Ayanna took them down to see some houses on the water.

The moment Ayanna pulled the car up to the Baislene-style home perched on the edge of the mountain overlooking the Caribbean Sea, Creigh could tell Willy was sold. The entire walk-through Willy couldn't stop gaping at the place. It needed work, but Willy almost liked that better.

"All right, this next house is for you, Creigh." Ayanna pulled the car to a stop in front of the large, dark wooden doors of what appeared to be a one-story Mediterranean-style home. "It's called Giai's Pearl and it's spectacular. And this is a highly desirable place, Contant Point, just a few miles from Cruz Bay. And the views, I mean you are going to die."

As they walked through the wooden doors in the open courtyard leading to the house, Creigh already felt that this place could be the one. Walking through the modern architecture, it was just what Creigh always wanted in a home. The indoor, outdoor spaces throughout would yield a perfect island style of living.

But it was the infinity pool on the back overlooking the sea that sold Creigh. Placing a hand on his heart he gasped, "This is it!"

"This is the complete selling point of this magnificent home. I mean, damn," Ayanna added, just as impressed as the Gang.

Creigh gaped. "I'm sold. How much?"

"It's a little over budget," Ayanna admitted. "But totally worth it."

"How much?" Karen asked.

"Two million."

Creigh whistled; it was way more than he wanted to spend on a house. It was too much to risk to spend a third of the money on a house. He still had other things he wanted to do with his money.

"I just don't—"

"We'll take it," Karen interjected. Creigh stared at her in confusion.

"We are doing this together, right?" Creigh nodded. "Then we are both paying for this. One mill each." Creigh was impressed as he agreed.

"Perfect," clapped Ayanna, clearly overjoyed by the sale of a $2 million house, the commission already calculated in her mind before they walked through the front door. "So that takes care of Willy and you guys. What about you?" Ayanna turned to John-Boy.

"Yeah, uh—" John-Boy seemed lost in thought, considering all they'd seen today. "I really just wanted to find a hut on the beach. I mean, just give me a hammock and a beer and I'm happy."

"Okay, I think I know the place."

It took them time to make it halfway across the island, but Ayanna finally slowed the car to stop and turned off the main road onto a gravel drive. "They don't have many of these left on the island," Ayanna announced. "Most have been bought torn down, and mansions built on the water, so we're lucky this one is still here."

As they walked up to the house, Creigh could see it all over John-Boy's face—he was sold. It was just what he wanted, complete with a straw roof and hammock between two palm trees on the private beach out in the middle of nowhere. It would be his own mini paradise and oasis. Creigh squeezed John-Boy's good shoulder, made him feel this level of happiness. It was knowing that all the anxiety, all the risk and fear, it was all to lead them to this moment. For each of them to have a life they truly wanted. It was all coming together—finally.

Everyone had something to celebrate that night at dinner, as they all sat around the long, wooden table on the outdoor patio overlooking Cruz Bay. Ayanna was thrilled to join them and seemed very content to sit next to Willy. Creigh even thought he saw Willy's hand on her knee at one point in the evening. Once they had all enjoyed the fresh Caribbean Lobster and Mahi along with the full course meal of salads, fruits and fresh vegetables, courtesy of the private chef Karen had hired for their last full night at the house, Creigh pushed back from the table and raised his glass.

"Cheers!" he said to the Gang. "I can't believe we are all here. All we went through, all we saw. I'm glad I have you as best friends and I would do anything for all of you. I assume each of you would do the same for me." All the boys nodded their heads in agreement. "Please, please look out for each other and maintain our oath and friendship forever." They all raised a glass to Creigh. "We did good and for that I am forever grateful that you all trusted me and stood beside me, especially you," he turned to Karen and took her hand. "Your support and all that you've done for us has been everything, it truly has. And in return, I want to give you everything."

The mood of the group shifted, as they all gaped at Creigh. Looking at their faces, he started to realize that everyone knew what he was about to do. Glancing at Karen, the red in her eyes as she tried not to cry felt it coming as well. Even Ayanna looked as if she knew.

Pulling the small box from his pocket, he knelt down on one knee, feeling his own eyes starting to burn with tears. "Karen—" his voice cracked. She grasped her hands around his shaking hands and smiled. "Will you?" was all he could get out.

"Yes, yes of course!" said Karen in a shaky voice.

Creigh breathed a sigh of relief and quickly took the diamond ring from its case and slid it onto Karen's finger before she changed her mind. As the ring slipped onto her finger it was like the final puzzle piece of his life was slipping into place.

Cheers erupted from the Gang, as they gathered around hooting and howling for Creigh and Karen. It felt right. It felt good. It felt perfect.

Everything was perfect.

31

A NEW FUTURE

The next morning, Creigh woke up and rolled over, taking Karen's finger in his hand, and turning the ring over her finger. *He was engaged*, he thought. He was going to spend the rest of his life with Karen, and he couldn't be happier.

"Good mornin'," Creigh whispered in Karen's ear as she started to wake up. "Want some coffee?" She nodded and stretched. "Stay here, I'll bring it to you."

In the kitchen, Creigh found Nicholas already up and pouring a cup. Something seemed off with him this morning. "What's up, man?"

"Uh, nothin'."

"Seems like something."

Creigh leaned back on the counter, waiting for Nicholas to open up.

"You think I can go back?"

"Back where? Home or school?" Creigh asked.

"School, man. I had a nice graduate position and scholarship. I don't want to give that up."

"Then why did you agree to do this with us?"

"Because you all are like brothers to me, family. I had to be there with you. I had to be there with you."

"Look, Nicholas, I always assumed you'd want to go back to school and with Kent behind bars, you should. You probably need to keep the money a secret though."

"Yeah, I figured that one." He shrugged and Creigh realized the money was never important to him. He only did this for them.

"I figured Danny will go home too, see his momma and all."

"Yeah, he mentioned it."

"Look, give it some time. I think we can live our lives, but we need to be careful. Kent is going to jail for life, I don't think we have to worry about him anymore. And hell, maybe we made some good investments, and it earned out," Creigh shrugged, trying to give Nicholas an out to use the money.

"Thanks, man."

"Look, we all deserve our own happiness." Nicholas nodded. "I know it's going to be hard today, after all, it's our last day here together." Creigh smiled, excited to tell Nicholas what he was able to pull off. "Which is why—" he paused for dramatic effect. "I've got us keys to an amazing place so we can spend the last few weeks of summer together."

"What? For real?"

"For real. Give us some more time to live it up. And then get your ass back to school."

"Dude, that's great news. I'm going to tell the boys."

"Sure thing."

Back upstairs, Creigh found Karen on the balcony, wrapped in a sheet, and gazing out over the water. Sliding up next to her, he handed her the steaming coffee.

"Coffee time, Coffee time!" Creigh softly sang to his future wife.

Karen responded by singing it back to him. This was their morning ritual.

The sun was slowly rising from the east and the scenery was breathtaking. In a few hours, they'd be packing up their clothes and starting a new future—together. Creigh played with the diamond ring on Karen's finger, elated with the idea of spending the rest of his life with her. He could see staying here on the island, spending his days with her, and having children. Anything was possible with Karen.

Two SUVs pulled up to the house a few hours later. Reluctantly, the Gang said goodbye to the Shark Cave and all the memories they had made there in the last week. But it was time to move on, to figure out the next phase of their lives now that they were rich. Creigh would marry Karen and live here for now. John-Boy would spend his time living the bum life on the beach and Creigh just knew Willy would make something of himself in this place. As for the others, they would all find their way, Creigh just knew it. He could feel it. That feeling he'd had that something was going to go wrong was finally lifted and gone.

After getting settled in their new home, having got in early due to the fact the owners agreed to that term considering they were paying cash, Creigh and Karen took off to the local market. While the place came fully furnished there were still a few things they needed. Karen focused on picking up some accent items to give the house a fresh touch, as well as some towels and toiletries. Then they focused on food, getting fresh fish and fruits from the local market to put together a delicious dinner together the first night in the new house.

When they got back to the house, they found the crew lounging out on the pool chairs, the infinity pool seamlessly connecting with the seas in the distance, the setting sun casting a warm glow across the horizon. After making dinner together, they all sat out on the patio. Every time Creigh took a moment to think about what they were doing, he couldn't believe this was his reality. That he was here, with all his friends and his fiancé. It felt like a dream.

"All right, I know it's no longer just a walk down the beach, but I say we go hit up Reed at the Beach Bar tonight. Anyone else down?" Danny asked. They all agreed, so after they cleaned up the kitchen, they all caught a cab over to the Beach Bar.

The Gang could see the glowing lights in the distance and hear the loud music as they walked up to the bar. It was a little after nine, as they greeted Reed and took their first round of shots.

"Cheers to the Shark Gang," Reed announced to the entire bar.

"Cheers," they called back.

It wasn't long before the Gang had taken over the bar with heavy tips and loud karaoke. It was as if everyone in the bar was there to watch them, to be their friend. Then Creigh saw Terrance and Nicholas entertaining the crowd by performing a line dance they learned many years earlier at a church camp. They all seemed to be partying as if they didn't have a care in the world and nothing but possibilities for their future.

The Gang continued to drink and party late into the night, Reed feeding them shots and stories that made them roar with laughter. As the night seemed to be calming down, Creigh gathered up the Gang to throw back a few more shots. Without any thought to it, Creigh and the Gang had drawn a lot of attention to themselves with their frequent tips and loud voices as they talked about the good ole days. Reed loved the stories, feeding them all more shots and asking for more stories, more shots until Creigh could barely focus his eyes on a single spot.

"To all our future stories and memories," Terrance announced on the ninth shot.

"To havin' each other's backs," shouted Willy.

"To the Shark Gang," Nicholas shouted, tossing back another shot. "Together forever!"

Creigh knew their lives were changed forever and this was just the beginning of their new future—together.

EPILOGUE

Throughout the night, the boys were loud but certainly not in a crude way. There was no cussing—just sheer happiness. Most of the Beach Bar crowd were entertained by the Hammerhead Gang's celebration.

Across the bar, a man sat alone at a small table in a dark corner. He was in a strategic location where no bathroom nor bar traffic passed his way. Only the accompanying waitress knew of his presence. He wore a black hoodie and had it snugged tight to his face. It was a bit warm for a hoodie but hoodies were common.

He was sipping on his fourth Smoked Old Fashioned of the evening. Glaring through his cloud of cigarette smoke, he continued to study the Hammerheads and their new friends.

Was he here by chance on vacation with his beautiful Bikini-Contest winning wife?

Was he here because he was on the run and had slipped away from the far-reaching grasp of the Feds?

Was he here to rape and kill another innocent 5-year-old girl? Or worse, had he already done the horrific deed?

Or was the billionaire here for vengeance on a group of punk young men from Florida?

Only time will tell...

Happy Shark Hunting for now...

THE END